Why cartoons have it better than us:

1. They never age. Ever. Wilma Flintstone *still* has a better figure than most of us.

2. Having a bad hair day? Just call the art department. Eight seconds with a new marker and you've got a fab new "do."

3. How else could you get a date with a superhero?

4. It's cool to be on a lunchbox. Very cool.

5. Doesn't everybody want their own theme song? With lyrics you'll be able to recite thirty years from now?

6. All it takes to shed ten pounds is…a decent eraser.

Books by Allie Pleiter

Steeple Hill Books

Bad Heiress Day
Queen Esther & The Second Graders Of Doom

Love Inspired

My So-Called Love Life #359

ALLIE PLEITER

Enthusiastic but slightly untidy mother of two, Allie Pleiter writes both fiction and nonfiction. An avid knitter and nonreformed chocoholic, she spends her days writing books, drinking coffee and finding new ways to avoid housework. Allie grew up in Connecticut, holds a B.S. in Speech from Northwestern University, spent fifteen years in the field of professional fund-raising. She lives with her husband, children and a Havanese dog name Bella in the suburbs of Chicago, Illinois.

My So-Called

Love Life

ALLIE PLEITER

Steeple
Hill®

Published by Steeple Hill Books™

STEEPLE HILL BOOKS

Steeple
Hill®

ISBN-13: 978-0-373-81273-8
ISBN-10:   0-373-81273-6

MY SO-CALLED LOVE LIFE

www.SteepleHill.com

Printed in U.S.A.

"For I know the plans I have for you,"
declares the Lord, "plans to prosper you
and not to harm you, plans to give you hope
and a future."
—*Jeremiah* 29:11

For Mandy.
Because when she draws, I see genius.

Acknowledgments:

Lindy and her world invaded mine without the slightest provocation. If someone had told me I'd spend hours thinking about wisecracking owls and the merits of a 7–10 split in bowling, I'd have laughed in their face. It's a wonderful world Lindy gets to live in. It would be wrong, however, to take all the credit for it. I had lots of fun, but I also had lots of help. Okay, the knitting part was all mine (I'm truly yarn obsessed), but thanks are due to the O'Reilly family for sharing their iguana, Chris, with me, and educating me on the facts of lizard life. The basics of my animation education came from Nancy Cartwright's delightful book *My Life as a 10-Year-Old Boy*. Voice actor Jesse Corti helped me in the mad dash to put authentic finishing touches on Lindy's work life. This book made me a particularly "high-maintenance" author and spouse, so were I to begin naming all the friends and family who help me, encourage me and endure me through the writing process, we'd all be here for sixty more pages…. To those who offer me support, you know who you are, and I hope you know how much I'm grateful.

Chapter One

America's Most Effective Date Killer

Let's get right to it, shall we?

Come with me to the corner table of the Treble Café, a trendy jazz club here in town. It's about eight-thirty at night, I've just had a killer fettuccine Alfredo—we are suspending all calorie counting for this evening, thank you very much—and are heading into the cheesecake portion of tonight's festivities. Soft rhythms and a smoky alto voice float out over the darkened room. Kyle, our man of the hour, has made it to crucial Date Number Three.

Which means I've just told Kyle The

Secret. The fact that Kyle has made it to the secret-revealing third date shows my irrepressible hope that somewhere out there is a man who can handle The Secret. Who will not be added to the long list of men who disappoint once learning The Secret. My nonstop, unsinkable faith that He May Be The One.

I'm holding my fork in midair, paralyzed by anticipation. I await the reaction for which I have long yearned. For which I have prayed in biblical proportions for what seems like forever.

Wait for it…wait for it… Come on, Lord, I'm ready….

"You're kidding!" he says.

This is not a good sign. Still, there is hope. I ignore the little red warning light flashing in the back of my mind. God is a big God. Kyle is an appealing man with lively brown eyes and hair that falls in that casual, almost-mussed way men somehow achieve effortlessly. He could still be The One. After all, he hasn't laughed yet, and that's a plus.

I should point out here that they *never*

believe me. I've never quite understood that. Would I make up the crazy thing I do for a living? Lie about something that has proven America's Most Effective Date Killer?

No, I wouldn't. Which is why I do my best to divert all "so what do you do?" questions until at least the third date.

Right here, right now.

Kyle's face is beginning the transformation I know far too well. My handsome, stable, sales manager of a date is mutating into a fourth-grade boy right before my eyes. The flashing red light has blossomed into a full-blown air raid siren. *Code blue!* This date is now in cardiac arrest. Those of you with delicate constitutions may wish to turn the page....

"Do it!" yelps Kyle with an awestruck expression. "Do *her.*"

Any and all hopes of an adult relationship have now flown out the window.

Why do they never understand that asking me that is like asking a dentist to drill your cavity for yuks? If you're a garbageman, I wouldn't ask you to haul out the restaurant's trash just so I could *watch.*

"Her" is what I do. It's not who I am. The average guy smart enough to graduate high school should be able to understand that.

I apply The Look. The "please don't ask me that" look. A last-ditch chance at survival, at diverting the fatal episode about to take place. Kyle sits back in his chair, eyes wide, arms crossed over his chest in smirking expectation. Just because I really like Kyle, I apply The Look a second time.

Nada. "Come on, just once. Do her. Pleeeeeeease?" Whining. An actual whine, from someone old enough to have a mortgage.

Condemned to watch this relationship dissolve before my very eyes, cursing the optimism that got me here, I go into ten seconds of *her.*

Maggie Hoot. The wisecracking owl from *Arborville,* the animated series.

Yes, *that Arborville. That* series. *That* owl. That's me. More precisely, that's my voice. Important distinction, as you will soon learn.

Once I become Maggie Hoot, all humanity is lost. Suddenly I am nothing else to Mr. Third Date except the voice of silly Maggie Hoot. Which means I am not a date, nor a woman, nor even human.

I am a cartoon.

And you'd no sooner date a cartoon than you'd date your grandmother.

It's gotten to the point where I can watch the transformation with an almost clinical detachment. Kyle stares at me for six or seven seconds, his brain trying desperately to reconcile the voice with the face before him. In his eyes, my face dissolves into Maggie's, my mannerisms become mere hints of hers. They think I'm just Maggie with skin instead of feathers. They try to make me laugh, somehow thinking that my laugh will be Maggie's hooting, trademark laugh.

Even if I've laughed just ten minutes before The Secret.

Then it starts. I hear about how much they love the show, how cool my job must be. All that stuff is nice to hear; gratifying both personally and professionally. I do understand how blessed I am to be working on a successful television show. I'm not an ungrateful idiot—I thank God every day for this job.

Oh, if it would only end there.

But it never does. I get about ten seconds of gratification until it slides into how cushy my life must be. How I must be raking in the bucks and spending my free time answering fan mail—ahem…no. How there must be almost no work involved in voicing a weekly animated series—*No!* The really awful ones ask me to do their phone answering machine messages—*Really, no!* Or call their nieces—*No!* Or their old girlfriends—*Absolutely Not!*

Sigh. My life's a hoot, that's for sure.

All right, enough of this social carnage. Fast forward two days to the place where Maggie really does exist.

Welcome to *Arborville*. Well, where we make *Arborville*. Treehouse Studios.

That woman over there behind the big shiny desk? That's Daphne, this year's thousand-watt enthusiastic intern. We get one of these every year, each one more peppy than the last. Thrilled down to their blue-sparkle toenail polish to be fetching coffee at *Arborville*. And where does our fearless leader Nigel put them? He's no fool: he puts those starstruck voices right where they can do the most good—and the least harm—answering the phones. Of course, we do usually have to do a little session on how to dress professionally and why it's best to stick to under a dozen earrings—stuff like that. Have you noticed how people assume all creative people are eccentric? Weird even? Lots of us are, but most of us are pretty ordinary folk who do laundry, eat peanut butter, go to the dentist and drink milk out of the carton when nobody's looking.

Voicing Maggie is a fabulous job, the job of a lifetime, really. But Maggie doesn't hug me when I need it or buy me birthday presents and she won't visit me in the nursing home. And if you ask my mother, Maggie can never be my husband, which means she can't make my life complete, "settle me down" or pave the way to adorable grandchildren. Yes, well, Mom's a bit preoccupied with my almost-famous-but-still-not-married status. I thank

God for every inch of distance between Boston and Los Angeles.

Back to Nigel, he is one of the reasons I stay in this business. Nigel Langdon is the brains behind *Arborville*. His title, which enthrones him as Treehouse's head artistic honcho, is "Creator." We all voice figments of Nigel's highly fertile imagination. Nigel's created a world of animals that truly mirror real people. *Arborville*'s birds, squirrels and mice are dead-on reflections of people you and I all know. They're geeks and hyper people, pessimists and geniuses, lovers and womanizers—only they're bird-izers, but that's what makes it so funny. Nigel's brilliant. Nigel calls the shots at Treehouse. Nigel's this decade's golden boy of animation.

Nigel's also an emotional basket case.

That human tornado over there with the exploding hair and torn leather jacket? The one who looks as if he's been up all night but is still bouncing around the office like a rubber ball? The only one outdressed by Daphne? That's Nigel. And, no, he hasn't had a bad time of it—he *always* looks like that. Nigel has the aura of a man continually on the verge of breakdown. If I saw Nigel calm and sitting still, I'm not sure I'd recognize him.

I adore Nigel for the tormented genius he is, pity the mess that is his life, and often yell at Jesus for not finding some way to get Nigel's attention.

Believe it or not, it's the Nigels of the TV business that keep me where I am. Some evenings, when taping sessions have gone long over schedule and we're all too wired up to go home but too fried to be with normal humans, Nigel and I end up "picnicking" on the lobby floor. We start by foraging through the studio kitchens for catering leftovers, but more often than not end up eating vending machine snacks and drinking too many sodas. Nigel has a heart so full of love and energy that he scares most people—himself included. His desperate pursuit of success and perfection drive him to both greatness and self-destruction. There I see a man, completely devoid of any peace whatsoever, sucking orange cheese-curl powder off his fingers.

"I want what you have." Nigel sighs, his spiked hair falling back against the hallway wall.

I tell him, again, about my faith, and he looks at me as if that is something he can never have. A prize he can never win. As if I am some kind of chosen one and he is not. We've had this conversation dozens of times. I tell him again that he will not mutate into Ward Cleaver if he lets God into his life. I tell him God loves him, not just me. Loves him just as he is, not when he cleans up his act. One day I hope to get through to him.

Have I mentioned my optimism problem?

One look at Nigel tells me that this morning will be no day for optimism. Nigel's mood swings make hormones look like hiccups. Some days the tornado is wild and wonderful and energizing; other days it is the force of destruction, taking everything and everyone down in its path.

From the look of things, today it's going to be Dorothy and Auntie Em and Toto....

I duck into the kitchen for more coffee. Not only do I find that Nigel's already downed the pot—I always know it's Nigel because he's one of those aggravating people who leaves two cc's of coffee in the pot because if he empties it he's supposed to make more…your office got one of those?—but Nigel follows me.

I glare at him as I yank the all-but-empty coffee carafe from the brewer. Nigel pretends to find something interesting on the ceiling. Having tasted this year's intern-blend of coffee—Daphne has been banned to purely fetching coffee and not ever making it ever, ever again—I know it's up to me to ensure further caffeination of my bloodstream. I silently inform God that I've developed quite enough patience and compassion this year, thank you, and open the cabinet door to fetch the grounds.

Nigel pushes the cabinet door shut again so he can glare into my eyes like a rabbit in headlights. "He's coming."

Chapter Two

Guess who's coming to Monday?

I pull the cabinet door back open. "Who's coming, Nigel?"

"The network. The *Suit*."

Stop right here.

"The Suit" is not a compliment. They are two words any creative person fears to hear. The network executive. If you've ever had one of these two-legged upper-management plagues come your way, you know what I mean. You may even be nodding your head right now, sympathy pouring out of your fingertips. You feel my pain. There are times when we like having the network send someone important down to see us. It means they notice us, they like us. In January, however, suits only mean trouble. "Suits" are usually clueless men in expensive clothes who have spent far too much time talking to the other expensive suits in the marketing department. Network executives are horrible creatures that would eat their own offspring if it might bring the ratings up. They come in, spout buzzwords, obliterate jobs, destroy lives and make vague recommendations sure to increase the misery of everyone within a six-mile radius.

I hate January. "When?"

"Today. Eleven."

Rats. We usually get more notice than that. "Where is it?"

"Your desk." Yes, I have a desk. I work for one single show, not running all over L.A. daily juggling six gigs like every other voice actor in this town. I am truly blessed. I even have an "office." It's tiny, but with an actual door and windows. This is unusual—no, *unheard* of—for my profession, but it's such "dream job" perks that make me suspect Nigel realizes what a royal pain he is.

"It" is the agenda. These guys always come to our table reads with an agenda. And a schedule. And stunning PowerPoint presentations designed to awe us into submission. Our Monday table reads are usually a familial affair, with everyone bemoaning their weekend or sharing some bit of great news. A completely agenda-free event. We all read the new script aloud and laugh because Nigel is so astoundingly brilliant.

I like Mondays at Treehouse. Mondays are the best of what we do, before the pressure of taping and everyone's creative ego kicks in. Mondays are full of possibility and laughs.

In comes Mr. Network to ruin all our fun. To remind us all that our jobs are on the line and there are seven thousand vastly talented people out there just itching to replace us.

He could be Moses in Armani and I'd still hate him. I don't even need to see him to know I don't like him. And, no, that's not judging, that's simply drawing on experience.

Nothing good ever came out of a network executive.

Not ever in January.

"I know you all hate me. You all hated me before I set one foot in this office, before one word came out of my mouth."

Well, I've got to give this one points for honesty. What Mr. Network fails to realize, however, is how many of the Mr. Networks come in here spouting "I know this is an adversarial relationship but I think we can all be friends" speeches. We've heard this one before, bub. Cut to the butchery and let's get this over with.

"And I'm sure you've heard all the lines, so I'll dispense with the usual hype. You want it straight, and you want me out of here so you can get on with your brilliance."

Okay, he has my attention. At least he hasn't dealt his business cards across the table like a Vegas card dealer. The last one did that. As if we'd all develop an urge to call him for private tutoring.

"The suit stops today."

"Come again, mate?" Nigel asks, pushing

up his round orange sunglasses. Did I mention Nigel was British?

"I do the suit thing because they expect me to. You expect me to. But I'll be here for five weeks and this is the last suit you'll see." Mr. Network takes off his jacket to illustrate his point. He loosens his tie with the look of a man who didn't much like having it on in the first place. I'm not sure I believe it. We've seen acts like this before.

"Oh, look," Jason Baxter says in a mocking voice as Mr. Network tosses his jacket onto a chair behind him, "the Evil Empire's trying to be one of us." Jason plays Dylan the Weasel on the show, and trust me, he's typecast. Sure, we're all thinking it, but Jason is the only one mean enough to say it out loud. While putting his feet on the table besides.

To his credit, Mr. Suit doesn't flinch. "Bottom line here is that *Arborville*'s ratings have fallen enough to make the network itchy about whether the show can hold its own against the four new shows out this season. Animation for adults—in prime time—is the hot market no one expected. A genre you all practically invented. One you've dominated for years. You guys did it first, and you did it better than anybody. That earned you the compliment of everyone breathing down your back. You can…"

"We did it first," Nigel interrupts, "and we'll keep doing it better than anyone." He has the sound of an insulted child about to pitch a fit. As you can imagine, he's not exactly a bastion of diplomacy at these things.

Dear Jesus, Prince of Peace, in Thy infinite mercy, deliver us from Mr. Network.

Somehow, despite my prayer, Mr. Network is sitting in my office two hours later. The jacket is still gone, as is the tie now, but he's gained a clipboard and takes annoyingly copious notes. At least it's not a laptop—the last guy kept typing so fast I felt like I was on an 800 line. Leo—the Suit's name is Leo Corbin, by the way— seems to want it straight. So I give it to him straight. "From where I sit, Nigel's earned the right to feel insulted. Every year they send us one of you guys to 'light a fire' underneath us and 'spur us to new creative heights.' All you really do is send Nigel off the deep end for a few weeks. Nigel is brilliant, he's *been* brilliant for four years. It's not like he's going to use up his recommended allowance of brilliance suddenly and we'll turn into a Saturday-morning cartoon. Guys like you make us miserable. I think you know that."

Leo smiles. "The dentist makes you miserable, too, but you still go twice a year."

"Poor metaphor, and who says I go twice a year?"

Leo picks up a package of dental floss I have somehow left on the corner of my desk. "Nobody who cares enough to floss at work skips out on their dentist." Don't tell me he's sharp and observant—he's just lucky and nosy. I never leave my floss out. Usually. Ick—now the guy knows my dental habits. These "get to know you" interviews are right up there with root canals in entertainment value.

"I understand what the dentist does. I go to the dentist of my choice." I snatch the floss out of his hands. "I fail to understand what it is *you guys* do. Except that you make Nigel more psychotic than he already is, we spend a month living on high alert, then Nigel comes up with something fabulous for ratings month, and everybody goes home. What I don't get is why you don't understand he'd come up with something fabulous whether you came here or not? Why make everyone miserable for no reason?"

Leo has the good sense to look offended. "Are you always this direct?"

"Hey," I reply, tucking my dental floss into the far back corner of my desk drawer, "You're the one going for total honesty. I applaud you for that, though. It's much nicer not having to pretend this is fun."

"Ouch. And they told me you were the nice one."

You know, I *am* the nice one. I make a point of showing compassion at work. And not just because I'm from Boston—we're not all bitter New York actor transplants, you know. Bostonians may drive fast and talk funny, but we're essentially a very friendly breed. It's my faith, though, that keeps me reaching out to these people.

Many of them are so thirsty for something deeper. I want to give them a glimpse of that. We've snuck a little bit of faith into quite a few episodes because of me and my late-night hallway floor sessions with Nigel. I took Jason the Weasel chicken soup last month when he had the flu. I pray for this cast every single day. I like to think of myself as a "What Would Jesus Do" kind of gal.

Leo is quiet. He leans back and picks up a Maggie's Pine Deli sign off my file cabinet. It's a real-life mock-up of the sign over Maggie's sandwich joint atop a spruce tree in *Arborville. Arborville* is, essentially, a New York neighborhood set inside a forest with animals instead of people. Dylan Weasel is the corrupt cop, Lillith Robin runs a beauty shop out of a dogwood tree, Edward Mockingbird can't seem to hold down a job in any tree—you get the picture. As Nigel is fond of saying, "it's our life, only leafier."

I didn't realize, until I saw Leo reach clear across my office, how tall he was.

Granted, it's a tiny office, but still, the man has to be over six feet. You would think that'd make him athletic looking, but it doesn't. Muscular, maybe, but not the jock type. He carries his frame with an unhurried ease. The kind of unconscious command that makes people instantly nervous. But, no, I'm not nervous.

I decide to change the subject on Leo. "Speaking of directness, you're awfully young to be an Agent of the Evil Empire. We usually get the over-forty crowd in here. How'd you get this stint at your tender years?"

He smiles again. I think he's enjoying this. He's not allowed to enjoy this. He's practically my age, which is way too young to have climbed up the network food chain on merit alone. He hasn't acquired that jaded, sell-your-own-mother-for-a-bigger-sponsor look.

He's having fun. Fun is *not* how this works.

"I asked for this 'stint.'" He mocks my choice of words.

"You asked for *Arborville?* You asked to be Nigel's personal tormentor? I always thought they drew short straws up at the network for that."

Leo gets up and twirls the sign around in his hands for a moment, not saying anything. I'm not really sure what to do with that, so I don't say anything, either. He replaces it in the exact position he found it. Without turning around, he says, "Could we drop the razor-edged repartee here and just have a conversation?"

Now I'm really not sure what to do with that. More awkward silence.

Clearing his throat, Leo sits back in the chair and attempts to put a foot casually over one knee. His long leg hits my bookshelf and sends a book—my Bible of all things—flying to the floor. Oh, great.

"Sorry." He leans over, picks it up. He thumbs through it. *Hands off my Bible, mister. That's my very favorite one.*

"I admit, I'm young for this job." His network tone is totally gone. "But I'm very good at what I do."

"Why'd you ask for *Arborville?*" I ask, mostly because I am too stumped to think of anything else to say.

"Because I love the show. It does things no other show does. Goes places other shows won't. Because Nigel doesn't cave to the network, ever."

These are all the reasons I love *Arborville*. Nigel eats controversy for breakfast, but it's not the shocking kind of controversy. It's the naked human condition "we're not supposed to let the world see that in us" kind of controversy. We accept the scared lonely failure that is Edward Mockingbird because while he's a dim-witted purple bird, he's the dim-witted bird in all of us we don't want anyone to see.

Nigel is the only man so acutely, painfully aware of the hole in all of us who hasn't yet figured out that it's a God-shaped hole. How can a man so brilliant see something so clearly and not see it at all?

"Why are you here?"

Leo had to think about this awhile. "It's my job."

"What's that supposed to mean?"

"My job is to take the realities of business and marketing and force them to invade the vision and rebellion of creativity. I wage tiny wars for a living."

"Meaning..." This guy's getting a little esoteric for me.

"My job is to tell the truth so *Arborville* can survive in the real world."

"We're doing just fine," I say defensively.

"No, you're not." His voice went from friendly to fierce in a heartbeat. He's a double threat—smooth and believable, but with an edge that lets you know he's not exactly on your side.

Our ratings have dropped, but ratings drop and rise all the time. Like roller coasters. We're supposed to enjoy the thrill ride, not get all panicky every time we slip a few points.

"Can you accept that I'm an *Arborville* fan, and I'm here because I want to be?"

"Okay." I can give him that much.

"That's all I need for now. Thanks, Lindy." The show credits list me as Melinda

Edwards. But I'd much rather everyone call me Lindy.

Leo called me Lindy. He did his homework.

I still don't trust him.

Chapter Three

Thumbing your nose at the Evil Empire

"So get out of here and go peck someone else to death!"

Nigel's voice comes in over my earphones. "Sorry love, you dropped off the end of that line a bit. Could you give it another go?"

Another go. This is "go" number fourteen. This is my job. Monday, when we all sit around and read the script as a group, is fun. Thursday, when we all begin the painstaking process of voicing lines onto tape, trying to match our delivery to the rough-drawn scene sketches art has already sent over, is *work*. I may be having a very funny conversation with someone, you may be laughing so hard you're snorting, but I can't see that from here. That fuzzy pink bird I just kicked out of my deli? She came and taped her lines hours ago. We've actually had guest voices on the show whom I've never even *met*. We'll probably have Brad Pitt on the show someday and I won't even be in the same zip code.

And *he's* watching.

I want to point out, here, that we would not be on "go" number fourteen if Leo Corbin weren't standing in the control booth behind Nigel. Usually, we've covered any nuances Nigel wants at the Monday table read, and I nail it at the taping, thank you very much. I never have to have more than three "goes" at anything.

Until today. Until *he* shows up.

Now don't get all analytical on me. Don't go suggesting "I wonder just who's more nervous?" Me or Nigel? No. No, I am not nervous.

A little on edge maybe. Would you want someone like floss-finding Leo Corbin staring at you while you work? I'm out here screeching like a hoot-owl—because…well…Maggie *is* a hoot-owl—and it's not attractive. It's not even cute.

But see that? I caught his eye. I caught you looking at me, Leo Corbin. And what does Mr. Network do? He does what all suits do: he takes notes. That's right, you just hunker down into your little notebook there and pretend that you don't know that I know that you were looking at me.

Nigel said he's sat through all ten hours of taping today. Only Nigel sits through all ten hours of taping. No sane person on the planet would sit through all the minutiae. Any executive type should be smart enough to know there are better places to spend his four-hundred-dollar-per-hour hours.

I am a professional. I do not get cranky and I finish my last three lines with perfection and cool, calm, expertise.

Why? Simple: banana.

At the end of each taping day, provided it's not late at night because Nigel decided to rewrite dialogue at the last minute—

which does happen—I treat myself to a milk shake. It's not the thick, dreamy concoction any New Englander knows as a frappe, but it comes close enough. As a matter of fact, it's probably good they can't make frappes out here—they're about a million calories when properly prepared. If you ask for skim milk and they use frozen yogurt, it can be just a few—hundred—calories. It feels beyond wonderful going down your throat.

Yes, I see Leo there by the door.

No. No-no-no-absolutely not.

No way am I bringing Leo along for my milk shake ritual. Not even to be polite. Not even to be "the nice one" and make up for my snide comments yesterday. Not even to...

"Hey, Corbin, do you like milk shakes?"

I did *not* say that out loud! Did I?

"Who doesn't?"

I *did* say that out loud. I stare at him because I cannot believe the words that just left my mouth.

"I'll even buy," Leo says. "As a personal thank-you to the voice of Maggie. Or an olive branch. Or a gesture of appreciation from the Evil Empire. Take your pick."

Since he's buying, it'd be poor form to decline, right? "Banana. I pick banana." We've all learned from *Star Wars* what happens when you thumb your nose at the Evil Empire.

Three blocks later, I find myself across the table at Hogan's Diner, breaking bread—or rather cheeseburgers—with the Evil Empire. And I know calling Leo the Evil Empire isn't fair. I can be a grown-up about such things. "Sorry about the Evil Empire stuff," I say as we slide into the booth. "Jason's a little harsh." If Edward Mockingbird is the purple bird in all of us we don't want the world to see, Dylan Weasel is the mean little weasel in all of us we wish the world never saw. I'm not only apologizing for Jason's—aka the Weasel's—words, I'm making retribution for my own. I'm not admitting that to Leo, of course, but it still counts.

Leo chuckles. He has a deep, lyrical laugh.

"A little harsh? I sat through Jason's taping. He swears like a sailor when he's angry."

"Jason's a one-take man. Thinks he's nailed every line on the first try. And, lots of times, he does. You don't get to be the world's favorite nasty weasel by personal warmth. And you know this is one of those businesses where, if you're supremely talented, you don't really have to be nice. Jason makes a good weasel because, well, he's mostly a lousy human."

"Still—" Leo points at me with a French fry "—I think everybody's got a good side." Leo has the kind of smile that catches you by surprise. Bright, quick and genuine. It gets under your skin before you have a chance to stop it.

"Why on earth did you sit through all of today's taping?"

"Is that so bad?"

"It's brutal. It's boring. Aren't there better ways to spend your expensive expertise?" That may have been a little sharp, but I really do want to know why anyone would do such a thing.

"It's raw data." Leo takes a big bite of

cheeseburger, as if those three words should be sufficient explanation.

"I don't get it."

I have to sit there and watch Leo chew, which sounds as if it'd be gross, but is actually a mini frozen-moment-in-time to really look at him. His hair is a dirty blond with just a little bit of wave to it. The kind with a dozen different colors in it that probably bleaches in the sun. He has a nice jaw. Strong. The green color of his eyes, like the sea glass from old soda bottles you used to find along the shore when you were a kid, could be warm and inviting or cold and merciless. I can see Leo giving an inspiring speech to whip a staff up into a frenzy of creativity. I can also see him cold and numbers-driven, giving a show the ax without flinching. I must have stared at him a full thirty seconds before realizing I've been gaping.

"The raw data," he continues with just the tiniest hint of a smile, "is the most important tool I have. I'm not involved in the show, so I don't jump to the same conclusions you all do. I'm not looking for evidence to support or disprove something, I'm just looking. Starting with the raw, undoctored information is what helps me be good at what I do. It helps me see things other people don't."

The waitress, a big, brassy, broad of a gal, saunters over to our table with the coffeepot in her hand. As she refills Leo's cup, she gives him a once-over just short of a wink. Then she looks at me. One hand parks on her hip. "You gonna eat anything, honey?"

I wrap both hands protectively around my milk shake, refusing to flinch under her "what's someone like him doing with someone like you?" glare. "No, really," I defend, "I'm fine."

"Thanks," Leo says, and the single syllable tells her to clearly but politely back off. That's command. Maybe suits have their uses.

We both shift in our seats. I attempt to restart the conversation. "I get the data thing, sort of. But tapings?"

"Your voices, the way Nigel works with them, which takes he chooses to use in the show and which he doesn't—that's all a kind of raw data. It just helps me understand."

I shake my head. "Come on, though, wouldn't an hour or two give you enough of a picture? Ten hours of taping is well beyond the call of duty. Your ears must be glazed over by now."

"Okay, it was a bit…daunting."

I give him the eye. "Daunting?"

"Okay, it took about ten cups of coffee and my notes have doodles in the margins. Were parts of it boring? Yes. But I learn things, and sometimes I have to wade through lots of boring data to find the one useful piece of data that helps me. Same as you—is it fun to give the same line twelve ways?"

"Not usually. Especially not when you're taping all alone."

"Exactly. But sometimes, on the twelfth take, you get just the right reading."

"Sometimes."

Leo takes a long sip of coffee. "How'd you get into this business anyway, Lindy?"

I swirl my straw to keep from looking at him. I've looked at him too much as it is.

"I started in college radio in Boston. Journalism. I was going to be the queen of hard-hitting radio news. You know. Shoving my tape recorder into the convicted felon's face outside the courtroom. Intensity. Drama. But they mostly needed someone to do the voiceover in commercials for the college station. Suddenly, I'm doing more announcing than reporting, and my journalism major is taking a back seat to the 'operators are standing by' and 'for a limited time only.' One day someone asked for a silly voice, and some part of me just burst into action. Like I'd been waiting my whole life to unleash those silly voices. One silly voice led to another, and voilà, I'm an owl."

"You're a very successful owl."

"As you can see—" I gesture to the mixed crowd around us in Hogan's Diner "—it gets me into all the best places."

"Hey," he replies, "I like this place. I may even adopt your milk shake habit, and when my cholesterol goes into the stratosphere it'll be your fault."

"I see no gun to your head."

Leo pauses for a long moment. "There's no gun to yours, either," he says quietly.

"Meaning…"

"Meaning I'm not the enemy. I'm not here to make you miserable or Nigel edgy. *Edgier.* My appearance is not the first step toward cancellation, okay?"

Nobody in our business believes that. "Nobody sends us one of you when things are going well. You have to know that you're the harbinger of doom here. How can someone as nice as you spend their professional life as a walking ultimatum?"

Okay, halt right here. This was supposed to be a diplomatic gesture, a quick beverage break to prove I'm not a nasty Hollywood diva. Polite, genial and over quickly.

How did we end up here?

How did I get to discussing my life's major turning point with this guy? I've talked way too much. He's like some kind of savvy reporter, drawing far more out of me than I was ever planning to say. And, to top things off, I just called him "nice," "walking ultimatum" and "harbinger of doom" in the same sentence. Way to make that first good impression, Lindy.

He should be throwing his money on the table and running out of here as fast as he can.

But he's not. He's not even looking pained. He's actually smiling. He's in no hurry to go anywhere. What's that mean?

Even after twenty more minutes of undeniably enjoyable conversation, I have no better grip on the situation. As we finish up our food and go, I keep banging up against the same impasse: I may have just met the only truly nice network executive in Los Angeles.

Then again, I may have merely met the smoothest. He did, after all, get a whopping load of background out of me with a single milk shake.

Got any idea which guy Leo is? I sure don't.

Chapter Four

The trouble with optimism

Even though it's 10:00 p.m., I'm relieved when the phone rings. Relieved because there's only two people on the planet who'd call me this late. Well, three actually, if you count Nigel, who's been known to call well into the wee hours of the morning on bad days—today clearly qualifies. This call is neither Nigel, nor my mother, but my friend Suzann.

"Lindy?" Suzann is one of those eternally perky people. Even at 10:00 p.m., even though I know she's been up since six, she sounds as though she just woke up from the best nap ever. The glass is always half-full for Suzann. One of those beautiful people who you'd love to hate but just can't because she's so incredibly nice. She has the sunniest disposition on the planet. While I find that annoying in most people, somehow it's one of the things I love about Suzann.

"Hey there, Suz. How'd the big meeting go?" Suzann is a local disc jockey—whom, by the way, people *do* love for their voices—but I'm not bitter or anything—who does the 10:00 a.m. to 2:00 p.m. shift on the smooth jazz radio station. Today her station had a corporate meeting to consider a format change. I'd be neurotic, wondering if my bread-and-butter vocal cords could suit the new format. Suz rolls with the punches. It doesn't bother her one bit. In my zany world, Suzann is my anchor. God gave her a daily allotment of peace just short of Mother Theresa's—nothing fazes this woman.

"We're changing to light rock. I'll be spending the next five years or so with Neil Diamond, Phil Collins and Mariah Carey."

"And you're okay with that?" I would

not be. I'm as change-averse as they come. Even though I'd classify it a short hop from smooth jazz to Phil Collins, I'd still be knee-deep in a pint of ice cream by now, agonizing over my now-shot future. I'm trying to ignore the pint of fudge ripple with the come-hither voice calling to me from the freezer as we speak.

"Fine. I was getting sick of the saxophone, anyway. Besides, I was beginning to think the only place people heard us was as background music in ladies' shoe stores." Suz is on her treadmill; I can tell from the rhythmic jolt in her voice. The treadmill. At ten o'clock at night. I'd give body parts to have her energy level. I'd probably have to give body parts to have her body-fat ratio. Did I mention she has great hair?

"Time slot?"

"Same."

"Manager?"

"New come February, but he sounds okay." See what I mean? Now me, I'd be in full-blown freak-out over whoever this new person will be with power over my future and happiness. Suzann, she's just sure everybody will be nice. And, for the most part she's right. She's got emotional Velcro of the best kind: a really nice person who has mastered the ability to fill her life with really nice people.

Any idea how you learn to do that? I seem to be emotional Velcro of the worst kind. Like the one moldy grape in your fridge that takes all its little grapey friends down with it. Not that I see myself as moldy. Really, I have a healthy self-esteem. I just seem to attract emotionally unhealthy people. Hence Suzann's high friend value.

I drag my thoughts back to the conversation at hand. "Playlist?" You probably think deejays sit around having fun choosing which songs we hear, decorating our air with their own fabulous taste in music. Wrong. Deejays are usually handed a pathetically short sponsor-, cash- or marketing-driven list of songs they must play. You know how you feel as though you're always hearing the same twelve songs on the radio? You are. If you're really talented and have a sizable following, you may get some artistic flexibility on your radio show. The other ninety-nine per cent of on-air talent are following marching orders.

"Too early to tell. But I can make a good guess based on what's out there. I should be able to sneak in a few good songs now and then if I behave myself."

"I'm glad it worked out okay for you, Suz." I'm staring at the rectangular wood-and-glass coffee table I bought in a fit of domesticity last week. Should I have gone with the round one? Would tile have been more practical? "Do you really think this table was the best choice?"

"Not that again. Yes, it's the right one. Will you stop it already? Tell me how was your week?"

"One word: suit."

"Oooh, lucky you. How bad was it?" They have "suits" in radio, too, you know. That, and the fact that Suzann's been through this a few times with me before.

"On a scale of one to ten? I'd give it a six."

"It's got a nice beat and you can dance to it?"

"He's got an annoying directness, he claims to love the show, and he bought me a milk shake." I move a brass bowl of decorative wooden balls—Suz's contribution to my home decorating episode—deciding it looks better on the other side of the table.

Suzann laughs. "They *all* claim to love the show."

"Yeah, but this guy really believes the line." I move the bowl back again. "He even told me he asked for our account."

"And the milk shake?" I hear her step off the treadmill.

"The invitation popped out of my mouth after taping. Involuntarily. I'm the nice one, remember."

"Aww. Well, you are. So, how was it?"

"Interesting." I kick back on my couch. "In a scary kind of way, but interesting."

"Okay," I hear her voice jolt as she sits down, as well, "give me the two moments." It's a game that Suzann and I play—naming the two best or most interesting or worst moments of any given encounter. We've been doing it for years.

"He goes for nerve-wracking honesty and he told me he's not the enemy."

"Before or after you were having milk shakes?"

"Why did I invite him to milk shakes?" I slap my hand over my eyes and cringe. "I never eat with the enemy. Why'd I say that?"

"Maybe because you need a wedding date in a few weeks? Guy in a suit would go nice with wedding cake." Suzann is engaged to Adam, the perfect guy, and she's getting married at the end of February. I'm thrilled for her. Really and truly. But there's a deep dark side of me that is so jealous it wants to scream.

"Now look, Kyle asked me out again, so I don't need to raid the network ranks to find a guy who knows what to do with a tie."

"Kyle called? After the secret-revealing date? That is news! I thought he acted like an idiot after you told him about Maggie."

"Well," I backpedal, "he was somewhat idiotic, but not completely. Given a few small improvements, some time to adjust to the new information, he may actually be okay. Maybe even wedding date material.

I know he goes to a great church, so there's another point in his favor. I've told God I'm willing to work with this one, so let's see where it goes."

"And the all-important date number four is…?"

"Church. Saturday night."

Kyle goes to one of those huge churches where they have multimedia everything and the pastor is on his fifth bestselling book. Kyle's been a gentleman all evening, and he looks quite sharp tonight. He manages to look trendy without looking overly concerned about his clothes. Groomed but not metro. That's a balance not often struck in L.A. Either a guy looks like a walking tornado à la Nigel, or looks like he gets manicures at the office. Kyle pulls off the look of giving it some thought but not too much. This, to me, is the unmistakable mark of an older sister who takes him shopping.

By the end of the evening my theory proves correct, as a trim brunette—the stay-at-home mom type with a pair of very clean kids in tow—bounces her way across the massive lobby to say hello. She's Danielle, Kyle's older sister. Told you he had a sister. Long years in the dating pool will teach you this kind of stuff.

He introduces me. Just me, not my job. Important distinction. I think this is going well.

Even Danielle looks as though she approves. "Hey, Kyle, that shirt looks good on you." She throws her daughter a knowing glance. "Doesn't Uncle Kyle look nice tonight?"

Kyle's thirteenish niece raises a skeptical eyebrow. "Yeah, not too bad, Uncle K." With a gulp I realize this is probably the niece Kyle wanted me to call as Maggie. We do have a chunk of the preteen market. These kids consider themselves too old for some cartoons, but don't realize that shows like *Arborville* still go mostly over their heads. This, if you're taking notes, is the distinction between "animation" and "cartoons." Cartoons show up on public television, weekday afternoons and Saturday morning. I work in animation. Prime-time network television, baby.

Right here's a good place to point out a very important truth about my job. People are almost never fans of *me*. They're fans of the show, or of Maggie Hoot in particular, but think about it: are you ever really fans of someone's voice? If they're a fan of the show, they enjoy how Nigel puts the characters together, how Nigel and the team of artists draw the show and how the characters are voiced—all combined. And yes, voice does play a huge—let me repeat *huge*—part in how a character comes to life. But your average television viewer doesn't separate that out from their enjoyment of the show.

If I had Maggie's wit, I'd have my own talk show by now. If I had Maggie's hair, I'd never have to slink out to the convenience store in a baseball cap again. If I had Maggie's figure...

I ask you: how pathetic is it when an owl—a rodent-snacking, head-spinning *bird* has better hair and a sleeker waistline than you? Real owls aren't witty or curvy.

Owls—the way God made them—are sneaky, sedentary, rather puffy and a bit untrustworthy in appearance. Like they've got a secret on you. I think that's where the "wise old owl" thing got started. So how'd I get hooked up with the one imaginary owl in all of creation who'd shame me at the health club? If I actually went to a health club, but that's for another day's insecurities....

Enough media education, let's get back to the social business at hand. Kyle's getting high marks for not having mentioned my avian counterpart. He's treated me just like, well, a woman and not an owl. *Oh, please Lord, let him not have said anything. Let this just be a great date, not a personal appearance.*

Kyle slips an arm around my waist as he touches his niece's cheek. She likes Uncle K—it's obvious. Hey, what's not to like? I'm sure that shirt wouldn't look nearly as good on the likes of Leo Corbin. "Thanks, Marcy," Kyle says, "I ought to let you two take me shopping more often."

I'm thinking *I* might want to take Kyle

shopping. For a suit to wear to Suzann's wedding perhaps?

Marcy rolls her eyes. "That's for sure."

I'm starting to enjoy this. I fit quite nicely under Kyle's arm, my shoulder tucking neatly under his. So what if he's a little bug-eyed about my job? It's a fabulous job. I'm almost famous. He appreciates what I do. He appreciates my talent.

"So," Danielle says, giving me a knowing glance, "Kyle tells me you're in television."

"I am."

"That's cool," says Marcy. I've obviously gone up a notch in her book. Kyle's hand tightens just the slightest bit. He's proud. Yes, that's it. He's proud.

"Well, I was thrilled when Kyle said you'd do the announcements for our upcoming Spring Break Bible school. The kids will just love it."

When Kyle said *what?*

Kyle's hand flies off my waist as if electrocuted. If I could have sent a few thousand volts coursing through his body at this moment, believe me, I would have.

"I…um…" I stutter. Kyle said *what?*

Danielle looks excited, as if she's chosen this moment to reveal to her kids just who it is Uncle K is dating. "Melinda is the voice of Maggie Hoot on *Arborville*, honey. That TV show you like so much. Uncle Kyle got her to do all the announcements for Spring Break Bible school. Isn't that great?"

"Danny," mumbles Kyle, "I sort of haven't asked her yet."

Let's freeze this precious moment right where it is and take stock of my situation. A nice date has suddenly turned into simply kissing up, some guy I hardly know is making promotional bookings for me with his big sister, and if I wish to turn down this little ultimatum—this slice of moral blackmail—I get to disappoint a young girl to her face. Oh, yes, this is turning into a stellar evening.

Wedding date my…*tail*feathers!

Chapter Five

Further trouble with optimism

"I'm an idiot. A complete idiot."

Kyle is standing in my doorway, after an excruciatingly silent drive home from the church where I had no choice but to graciously offer my voice—*mine,* not Maggie's—to the service of Our Lord for Spring Break Bible school.

"Well, yes." I'm still hopping mad. Justifiably hopping mad.

Which is, of course, when Kyle does "the thing." It's this gesture men seem to innately have, a sheepish hand-in-hair thing. And it works. Every time. Where, where do they get this ability? This talent for looking extraordinarily adorable when apologizing for something stupid they've done. I think Hugh Grant got them all into an auditorium when we weren't looking and taught them how to charm us after whopping lapses in judgment. One hour ago, those eyes didn't have that dreamy I-need-you-to-make-me-a-better-man quality. One hour ago they were big brown pools of manipulation. Now, they're so deep and remorseful I can barely stand it. How do they do that to us?

Why are we so willing to let them?

"Well," I capitulate under the spell of that look, "maybe just a guy with supreme idiotic tendencies."

"It was a dumb thing to do." Kyle leans against my doorway, looking as if he'll launch into the "you complete me" speech from *Jerry Maguire* any second now.

"Yes."

"My sister, she's just so…so successful. Everybody at church loves her and she knows everyone important. She's always running things and leading stuff and has this fantastic marriage. I just…I wanted to show her up, you know? Show her I knew important people, too."

Aww. Did you hear that? I'm important. To err is human and all that, right? There's about a dozen Bible verses to back me up on this.

Kyle touches my shoulder. "Thanks for saying you'd do it anyway. After I was a jerk and all."

"I'll expect a very nice dinner after the taping next week."

He smiles. "You name the place." His finger plays with a bit of embroidery on my sleeve. Tingles. Actual tingles. Wow, I'd almost forgotten what those feel like.

"I…um…" I fight the urge to shake my head to clear it, "I can't do it as Maggie, you know. She's copyrighted. There's no way I'd get permission to do that kind of thing."

Maggie comes out of my mouth, I give her life, but I don't own her. I can make all the public appearances I want as Lindy Edwards, but I can't sit there and say anything you want as Maggie Hoot. If you want Maggie to push your product, then you have to shell out the big licensing bucks to our studio to buy the rights to Maggie's endorsement.

"It's okay," he says, but you can see the disappointment in his eyes.

At this point, I should say, "hey, bub, it's *me* that's important, not the cartoon," and kick him out of my proverbial diner like the bossy owl I embody.

But I don't. "But hey, maybe I'll ask anyway. I mean, I'm important and all." Who am I kidding? Now I'm the one trying to impress him? How do they *do* that to us? *Lord, what were you thinking when you made this whole male-female thing up anyway? Didn't you realize how badly we would botch this?*

"That'd be so great. So great."

We stare at each other for a moment. Me, basking in my importance. Him, basking in his adorableness. He takes my hand and runs his fingers over it, as though it was something smooth and lovely.

"I'll pick you up Saturday at five-thirty. Danny said it'll take about an hour in the church sound booth and then we'll go to dinner wherever you like."

"Okay." He's doing things to my hand that make any more than two syllables impossible. With a feathery brush of his fingers against mine, he turns down the hall toward the elevator.

I push the door shut and lean my forehead against it.

A fifth date. An actual fifth date. You've figured out by now what a huge thing that is?

Yes, it's to record announcements I should never have been blackmailed into making, and yes, he's been a idiot, and yes, I'll never get permission to do them as Maggie, but...

...but fifth dates for Lindy Edwards are about as frequent as snow in L.A., and it's five short weeks until Suzann's wedding, so we're going for it.

Since it's only ten-thirty, I do what comes naturally: I call Suzann to dish about the date. I happen to know she's home and not out being her perky energetic self because the radio station asked her to host a Sunday morning jazz brunch tomorrow. Which means she's home giving herself a manicure, pedicure and facial.

Suzann picks it up on the second ring. "Soooo, how was church with Kyle?"

"You do have caller ID, don't you? I mean, you wouldn't just answer the phone like that unless you knew it was me? What if it was Nigel, saying I'd collapsed at a promotional appearance and you needed to come to the emergency room and sign my death certificate?"

"Oh, am I your 'in case of emergency notify' person? That's so sweet. I'm touched, really I am. Sooo, how was church with Kyle?"

I swerve past the pint of fudge ripple in the freezer to fish a sugar-free fudge pop out of the box right next to it. "Before or after he shanghaied me into doing the Spring Break Bible school announcements?"

"You mean as Maggie? Oh, he didn't."

"Told his sister I'd do it before he even asked me."

"Sleazy," Suzann comments. "I'll bet that ended the…hey, wait a minute…you didn't say you'd *do* it, did you?"

"Well, I sort of…"

"Lindy…"

"He did the cute 'I'm sorry' thing. Told me he was trying to impress his sister." I rip the paper off my fudge pop.

"And you fell for it, didn't you?"

"You should have seen how cute he was. And come on, Suz, he's a fifth date. That's got to count for something."

Suz is not impressed. "Is he dating you or booking your personal appearances?"

"It's been so long since I've been on a fifth date I'm not sure I care which it is." Which is, of course, a lie. I know it, Suz knows it—you probably already know it by now. I'm aching to be loved for more than the sum of my vocal cords. Aching enough to give Kyle the benefit of the doubt, at least. Besides, a fifth date would be a world record for me. I sink into a chair and kick off my less-than-sensible-but-still-churchworthy date shoes. I wore *nylons* for this guy; he must mean something to me on some level.

"So," Suzann says into my ear, "aside from his exploitation tendencies, let's hear it: two moments, please."

I mull over the evening. There were several moments, but in the back of my mind I'm always picking out the two best because I know Suz will ask. "When the praise band kicked in and he started singing. That's always a weird moment, you know, when you are supposed to be singing without listening to the people around you but you're listening anyway while trying to sing inconspicuously so that 'Amazing Grace' is directed at God, not your date? He has a good voice. Ten-or-ish. The kind you'd like to hear sing a Paul McCartney ballad."

"Mmm. Nice. Good voice is always a plus. And?"

"He took my hand when he said good night. This guy has the most amazing hands."

"You always say that. You've got a thing about hands, Lindy. It's weird if you ask me."

I point the fudge pop in the air at her— figuratively speaking, of course. "It is *not* weird. Hands are very revealing. He just sort of brushed my fingers very gently. Sweet and tingly."

"Tingles are good. Tingles count for a lot."

"Yep."

"Tingles only barely make up for the fact that he assumed you'd trot Maggie out for his church's microphones. Has the man never encountered the concept of copyright?"

"Look it was a dumb thing to do, but he knows it. He said he was sorry about a dozen times."

"Oh, and that makes it okay?"

"That makes it worth a second chance. How many guys do you know who will admit to being, and I quote, 'a complete idiot,' on the fourth date?"

"Okay," relents Suzann, "but I'm still saying my prayers and keeping my cell phone on."

Chapter Six

The virtues of discreet pigtail removal

It's a good thing Kyle asked me to tape on Saturday night, because the third Friday in January has been booked indefinitely for me. Only Jesus's return could drag me away from the Crystal Theater on the third Friday in January. There are no dates, no company, no companionship; just me, the L.A. County Cartoon Festival and the largest available portions of both popcorn and diet soda.

I love animation. My profession is reaching new heights in the last decade that I'm sure even Walt Disney couldn't have imagined. More animated feature films—of more spectacular intricacy and artistic splendor—have been produced in the last ten years than at any point in cinematic history. Cable TV has birthed more homes for animated shows than ever before. We're at the zenith of the art form. And who knows where the computer will take us from here?

But my secret love, my guilty pleasure, is cartoons. Pure, hand-drawn, guffaw-producing Saturday-morning cartoons. All the old shows that kept me glued to the couch when I was a kid, all the hokey theme songs you and I can recite every verse of, the funny voices and cheesy sound effects, those characters we had to have on our pajamas and first-grade lunch boxes. Remember that? Tying a bath towel around your neck and pretending you were "Super-*whatever?*" Tearing around the block on your bicycle, tricycle or training wheels pretending you were "Speed-*whatever?*" *That's* what makes my heart sing. In those color-blasted half hours my soul fell in love with the inked character. With the visual alchemy that is animation.

For me, the L.A. County Cartoon Festival is like opening up my personal biography. It all comes back with every show they put up on the big screen. It's all I can do not to show up in my pajamas with a box of Cocoa Puffs (I've thought about it). I go every year, because it is a near-sacred thing to me. And I go alone, because it is a near-sacred thing to me.

The seventh row, right-hand side. Always fourth or fifth seat in. Popcorn on the left, soda on the right. I wear clogs so I can kick off my shoes and tuck my socked feet underneath me, curled childlike on the red chenille chair. One inhale as the lights go down and it all comes back. I am seven again, and it's bliss.

Over the years, I have noticed other devotees at this annual pilgrimage to our childhoods. There is a "regular" crowd of sorts—a few people I know from the industry, others who just share the mutual love of cartoons and a few others who don't look old enough to have seen any of this on television but share my awe anyway.

There's the fiftyish couple who always sit behind me to my left. There's a few artistic-looking Nigel types who come together but scatter solo around the theater and take notes. There's the three women who always show up in sweatshirts with characters on them—I'm guessing this is an annual "Girls night out" for a trio of lifelong best friends. There's that tall guy who's been here for the last three years. He always sits in the first row, but he's not here yet.

Oh, no.

It's been hiding in the back of my mind for weeks, lurking like a badly planned prank. It goes through my system like ice water once my brain snaps—or rather, slams the pieces together.

No! This is sick and twisted. I'm jumping to conclusions for reasons even I can't explain. It isn't. It couldn't be.

It is.

That tall guy walking down the aisle to his seat in the first row is *him. Leo* him. You knew it would be him, didn't you? You figured it out three paragraphs ago when I started gushing about how much this night means to me. "Oh, I bet *he* turns up," you said to yourself.

Thanks for the warning. You could have told me to sit somewhere else this year. You could have stopped me when I gave in to the obviously psychotic impulse to tie my hair back in pigtails. Intervened before I shrugged into the sweats, baggy wool socks and stretched-out old turtleneck I am currently wearing. But, no. Instead, I am the visual definition of female patheticness, if that's even a word.

And Leo Corbin is staring right at me.

You're enjoying this, aren't you? Well, I'm glad one of us is, because right now the entire United States military is marching through my stomach. Double time.

It takes him several seconds to recognize me. That would be due to the fact that I probably more closely resemble a fifth grader home sick from school than a successful voice actor. I barely even have any makeup on. For a few seconds I harbor the hope that he won't recognize me. But you already knew that hope was lost. His face changes completely when his brain makes the connection.

Mercy! That smile should be outlawed in twelve states.

Please, Lord, don't let him come sit with me.

Leo throws his jacket down on the chair next to him, still staring at me. Wondering, I'm sure, if I've taken ill or had a recent death in the family. Thinking, I'm certain, that any woman my age in pigtails must have serious issues.

I want to die. Or become invisible. Or find a stunning new outfit and hair-care products in the ladies' bathroom at intermission.

Now really, how stupid is that? I'm not interested in Leo Corbin. He's a colleague, and if he can't get his high-priced brain around the fact that how I dress on my own time is my own business, that I'm here to watch something, not be seen, then that's his problem.

Yeah, I don't believe it, either.

He hoists his soda, as if toasting me. I toast back. And exhale when he turns and sits down in the front row. I offer up a quick prayer of thanks that he didn't attempt to come sit with me.

Not that it makes a difference.

It seems like only a heartbeat before intermission yanks me back to grown-up reality. And, no, I pulled my pigtails out because they were bothering me, that's all.

Now what? Do I walk over to his seat and make small talk? Do I ignore his presence? Let him walk over to my seat and make small talk?

I opt to stay put, running my fingers through my hair as casually as I can.

He's getting up. Wow, how do guys get jeans to fit like that? He's coming straight over here.

"Hi, Lindy. Want me to get a refill for you?"

Ah, confirmation. Festival regulars know that they give free popcorn and drink refills all night long. I'm not imagining it—he's the guy who's been coming here for years. It poses a dilemma, though. I'm holding one whopping bucket. Do I admit that I've chowed through a gallon of popcorn and would gulp down more if given the opportunity? Does that make me free spirit or glutton? Do I care? Do I want him to suspect I care?

Could I be more pathetic?

"Sure. No butter, though." Ooo, Lindy, good save. No butter makes you look controlled but open to abundance.

I'm still congratulating myself when Leo returns with my refilled bucket. "You want to grab a cup of coffee after?"

"Maybe." Controlled, but open to abundance. That's me.

"Okay, we'll see." Leo walks back to his seat as if we've just discussed the salt content of the popcorn, not had what could be construed as an actual social encounter.

Leo looks cool and calm.

Me, I'm on my third handful of popcorn by the time Leo sits down.

Chapter Seven

A monumentally bad idea

"And then, the part where the hammer comes down…"

"And he flies backward into the cliff…"

"I could see that a million times and still laugh like a hyena." Leo stirs cream into his coffee, evidently unaware that he *is,* in fact, currently laughing like a hyena. It's fun to watch. What do you know? Get this guy out of a suit and he turns out normal. This is a new Leo. A less slick but still-charming Leo. A Leo who eats Cap'n Crunch like he was still in college.

"I'm glad they sell coffee here," I say,

"That way I can tell people I had coffee with the network and not be lying."

"So, if you leave out the Cocoa Puffs part, it's not lying?" Leo narrows his eyes and points at me with his spoon, and you can just tell this guy was captain of his debate team in high school. Or class president. Or, perchance, in the Future Network Executives of America club that met on Thursdays in the AV lab.

"No, it's merely selective information sharing." I still can't believe we ended up here at all. It was a goofy impulse to poke our noses in here, but the place has been in the news for months and who could resist a bowl of cereal after a night of cartoons?

Yes, cereal. I'm eating cereal with Leo Corbin. We started out going for coffee and ended up here, at the Soul Bowl Cereal Bar. That's right, a late-night joint where mild-mannered adults can go dive into a bowl of juvenile sugarcoated anything and feel trendy instead of pathetic. If we eat it on our couches at 11:00 p.m. on a Friday night, it's pathetic. If we eat it at the Soul Bowl at 11:00 p.m.

on a Friday night, we're on the leading edge of a food trend. They've got everything in here your mother would never let you eat when you were a kid. And you can combine it!

"What's with the shirt?" The bowling shirt Leo has on is retro-garish enough to win a spot on *Antiques Roadshow*. It's green and yellow, and has some odd team name on the back. "Lenny?" I ask, pointing to the name embroidered on the front. "I really don't see you as a Lenny."

Leo tugs on the fabric with both hands, showing off the splendor of his attire. "Gift from my sisters. They think it's funny to scour the world's secondhand stores to find bowling shirts for me with anything even close to my name. I'm garnering quite a collection."

Sisters. Plural. Duly noted. "Unique."

Leo raises an eyebrow. "No, odd. But it's grown on me. Long way from a suit to—" he tugs his collar "—this. Part of the appeal, I suppose."

I lean in a bit, lowering my voice. "You're not going to tell me you have a secret crime-fighting alter ego who saves the world with a well-thrown bowling ball, are you?"

Leo bursts out laughing. The guy has a great laugh. You hardly ever notice someone's laugh for positive reasons, but Leo's laugh is so hearty and so genuine it practically dares you not to join in. Definitely not something I generally attribute to network types.

"That would be cool, wouldn't it?" He adopts a deep superhero voice. "Look, up in the sky...it's Pin Man!"

Cocoa Puffs and coffee with Pin Man. At 11:14 on a Friday night. This is crazy.

Leo is nice.

I know you figured that out two chapters ago. Believing Leo is nice is such a monumentally bad idea, so totally unwise, that you can't really blame me for hiding it from myself.

He loves cartoons—and I mean *loves* them in the same way I do. He's seen me in sweats and no makeup—other than what I could forage out of my purse in the ladies' room during intermission—and not run the other way. He's done seven dead-on imitations of my favorite characters. He's done an eighth that he's really deluding himself on—it's truly horrible—but I'm willing to look past it.

Ah, but Leo is also part of the Evil Empire. Holding my professional future in his analytic network hands. I can never forget that this guy can ruin me.

"I can't believe I want a third bowl," he says, starting to get up. "But I do. I'd knock over a crowd of..."

"Whatareyougoingtodowith*Arborville?*" I blurt out. I can't stand it anymore. I have to know.

Leo sits back down, slowly. "What am I what?"

"What are you going to do with *Arborville?*" I repeat, trying to sound as if it's an acceptable question instead of a gargantuan breach of professional conduct. "Straight," I add because it sounds strong and emphatic, even over a bowl of Cocoa Puffs, "I want it straight."

"The 'straight' is that I don't know yet."

"Are you going to cancel us?" I figure it's okay to go for the jugular here. He's seen me in pigtails so it's not like I have any dignity to loose.

"I don't know yet. I know I don't want to drop the show."

But you could. He didn't say that, but it's there, hanging at the end of his sentence for all the world to see. "You don't want to cancel us. That sounds way too much like 'this is going to hurt me much more than it hurts you.'"

"Have you been this cynical all your career? I can't have been the first network guy to rattle your cages. Why are you getting so worked up about this before I've said one word about my conclusions?"

Leo has a good point. I am really rattled. Much more than the last time they sent down a suit to analyze our standings. Which leads me to the inescapable fact that it's not Leo's job, it's Leo.

But that's not true, either. Tensions have been rising at Treehouse over the past year. We used to laugh in the face of whatever guy the network sent down. Now we're scared. We're all hearing the thin whisper of "how much longer are we going to get

away with this?" that lurks in the unconscious of everyone who's landed their
dream job. *Arborville* is my dream job. I've
wanted to work in animation since that day
in college when the silly voices burst out
at me. And *Arborville* is so much more than
a cartoon. It uses animals to get to the very
heart of what makes us human. We make
people laugh, we shake them up a little, but
it's the kind of shaking that makes them
think. I'm proud of our work. I don't want
it to end. Every once in a while I wake up
in a cold sweat at night, certain in my
knowledge that surely something this
fabulous can't last. Everyone at *Arborville*
has been living our dream. Leo looks far
too much like the alarm clock that just
might end it all.

This whole panicked thought process
must have shown on my face, because Leo
got a very intense look in his eyes. "Look,
Lindy, I already told you I asked to come
here. I meant it when I said I don't want to
see *Arborville* dropped. I'm here because
I don't want some number-crunching jerk
to jump to a wrong conclusion just because

the network's a little nervous right now."
He grabs my hand for emphasis. "I'm on
your side. Remember that."

He grabbed my hand.

He grabbed my hand. I don't think he even
realized he was doing it, but it's gone through
both of us like a thunderbolt. We both freeze.
His hand is on mine. Perfectly still, with
about a thousand and one nerve endings in
overdrive. I don't know what to do. I don't
think he knows what to do. Suddenly there's
a mile-wide crack in Leo's cool, calm
demeanor. Now what? Now WHAT?

"I'm…I'm on your side." Leo brings his
hand back slowly. I'd even say reluctantly.
We're both trying to pretend that what just
happened didn't happen. Which is dumb,
because whatever just happened happened
in huge proportions. He felt it. I felt it. I
wouldn't be surprised if half of Los
Angeles felt it.

"I—I know." I stutter, because my brain
has blanked out as if a flashbulb went off
behind my eyes. He must have felt that.
That whatever when he touched me. He
looks like I feel so he must have felt it.

Leo and I bumble our way through another ten minutes of small talk and cereal. We are both so caught off-guard that all conversational skill seems to have left us. It's absurd; we're trying to fake a casual calm when our minds are racing a thousand different directions.

I need a minute to think over what just happened.

No, I need a *week* to think over what just happened. It's feeling as if it would take an hour of prayer, four conversations with Suzann and a dozen journal pages to figure out what to do with this.

Too bad we're down to our last spoonfuls of cereal.

"Well," says Leo, "It's getting on the late side." His tone of voice sounds as though he'd have given anything to have something more clever to say. Believe it or not, I'm pretty sure cool, calm Leo is even more startled than I am—which is saying something.

"Yep." Speaking of needing something more clever to say...

Leo tips his bowl as if to demonstrate its empty status. "We'd better get going."

I don't want to leave things here, but I haven't the faintest idea what to do about it. I'm stumped.

Once out the door, the awkwardness just gets worse. "Where are you parked?" Leo asks.

"Over there," I say, pointing to the left. "You?"

"Over there." Leo is, of course, pointing in the other direction.

"You want me to walk you to your car?" Leo's actually stubbing his toe on the ground like some junior high kid.

Yes. No. Maybe. Desperately. "I'm okay. It's right at the end of the block."

"Well, all right then." He picks this moment to say the absolute worst thing: "See you Monday."

See you Monday. That's pretty much the whole problem, isn't it? "Monday it is. Hey," I add impulsively, not wanting tonight to end on a Monday note, "the cereal thing is pretty fun, hmm?"

Leo laughs a little. "It is."

Another awful pause. "Okay then, well, I'll see you."

Leo stuffs his hands in his pockets and starts to turn. "Good night."

Ugh! This is going so badly. Where's the clever parting quip, the one that hints at everything and nothing at all, you know, the *line?* I'm on a television show with enough writing awards to fill two fireplace mantels and I can't come up with a decent parting line? If there's some piece of splendid Maggie Hoot dialogue to fit this moment, I've lost all mental ability to retrieve it. Where's a good writer when you need one in real life?

"Good night." It sounds sick the way I say it. Talk about your lost moments. I turn toward my car, fighting back the urge to whack my hand against my forehead.

We've both taken two or three steps when he says, "No."

I dare to crane my head around to find him standing there, staring at me with the oddest look on his face. "What?"

"No," he repeats, taking a step toward me. My breath stops. "No." His voice gains momentum as he repeats it. "I'm not going to stand here and…and pretend I didn't touch your hand back there."

Oh my.

Chapter Eight

Complicated wouldn't begin to cover it

Now what?

Leo stares at me, so far from the consultant persona right now that my brain is straining to fuse the two personalities.

"Um…" *Oh, yes, Lindy, you communicate for a living.* Insects are more articulate. Most *garden vegetables* are more articulate.

"Yeah," Leo sighs, running one hand nervously through his hair.

"We should probably ignore that." I try to keep the astonishment out of my voice.

"It does kind of ruin protocol, doesn't it?"

"Um, yes."

"This is a bad idea, right?" He doesn't look very convinced.

"Network complications aside—and trust me, those are big enough, Leo—I'm a Christian." I take a seat on a bench near my car. "I'm a person of faith. I don't ever do…" I gesture vaguely, unable to come up with a suitable noun for whatever "this" is. "My faith is too important to me to start things up with someone—" I look up at him "—no matter how nice, who doesn't share that. It's just not a good idea."

"I know." He's smiling.

"You know?" *Don't do this to me Lord.*

Leo sits down. "You don't think I'm the kind of guy who goes around stalking women at animation festivals to get them over Cap'n Crunch do you? I pray long and hard before I eat cereal impulsively with someone."

It is a full ten seconds before I catch the implausibility—and the revelation—of his comment. One cannot of course, pray long and hard before doing something impulsive. Hence the definition of impulsive, meaning something done without forethought. Like, for example, breakfast cereal. But he said "pray long and hard," meaning he knows what that means. "Oh." Once again, my dialogue skills continue to astound.

"The Bible I knocked off your desk was my first clue, but a long conversation with Nigel gave you away easily. I admire the way people on the show know about your faith and respect it. That's a hard thing to pull off—especially in this business."

"Tell me about it." Wait, he's talked to Nigel about me? Nigel's spoken highly of my faith? I'm straining to keep my chin off my knees.

"I haven't pulled it off well," Leo continues. "At least not nearly as well as you have. People in my office know, but they'd certainly never speak of me in the warm way Nigel and some others do about you. Good Christian girls are nice. Good Christian girls who love *Underdog* are…well… a rare find."

Compliment my hair, and I like you. Compliment my interpersonal relationships, and I really like you. Gush about the authenticity of my faith, and I'm your new best friend. "I've got it a bit easier. You, well think about it—it is kind of hard to combine good Christian values with network heartlessness. You can't be the portent of the Evil Empire and a pillar of compassion at the same time."

Leo swivels on the bench to face me. "Have dinner with me tomorrow night. Real food this time—no milk shakes, no cereal."

Can I believe this? Do I accept? Thankfully, I remember that tonight is Friday, which means tomorrow is Saturday, which means I'm having dinner with Kyle.

"I can't. I'm…busy." It came out all wrong. It sounds just like the one thing I don't want it to say: like I have another date. You'd think the one chance in my life I get to say "I can't have dinner with you, I have another date that night" would feel victorious. It feels awful. Leo is quiet for a moment and it feels even more awful.

"I don't want the next time I see you to be Monday morning," he says quietly.

How on earth am I supposed to know if this guy is sincere and not on the network make? He looks so nice. He sounds like such a nice guy. Fireworks—not tingles, *fireworks*—go off when he touches me. But it could all be smoke and mirrors. I don't really know the guy. Really. You know what they say: too good to be true usually is. I need time. I need a chance to see if this guy's for real. Inspiration strikes. "Hey, I have to walk Nigel's iguana on Sunday afternoon. Wanna come?"

Leo looks baffled. "Did you just invite me to go iguana walking?" he says slowly. "Iguanas walk?"

"Nigel's does. Well, it's more like sunbathing on a leash. She's been sick so he wants her to get time outside every day. Nigel treats Marilyn like a dog—a very green, very unusual, very spoiled little dog. He's in San Francisco for the weekend, and I'm on lizard duty. You'll get a kick out of her." Nigel's Marilyn Monroe obsession extends clear out to his pets. Just telling Leo about Marilyn is proving extremely funny—the "you've got to be kidding" look on his face is entertaining. Can you imagine the look on Leo's face when he gets a load of Marilyn's rhinestone harness and pink leather leash? Can you imagine Leo on the other end of that leash? I feel outlandish walking that creature. I'm cracking up inside just picturing Leo on lizard duty.

Leo clears his throat. "How could any intelligent man turn down the chance to walk a lizard?"

Chapter Nine

Fiber psychiatry

The store's sign says that Fiber Content opens at 10:00 a.m. on Saturdays. That is *if* Sophia, the marvelously artistic woman who owns this yarn shop I frequent, makes it to work on time. Sophia is one of those quintessential West Coast kind of people who have decided punctuality is overrated. I love her. The control freak in me marvels at her. The artist in me admires her. Fiber Content runs on "Sophia time." In a world where my work is measured down to the millisecond, Fiber Content is a place to leave it all behind.

Fiber Content, I might add, is also a lot cheaper than therapy. As a matter of fact, I feel like it *is* therapy, in a way. Everyone who knows me knows that when I have a thorny problem to work out, I do it at Fiber Content.

Today, I may just buy the entire store. Which is why I have asked Suzann to meet me here. Suz will grab the credit card out of my hands when the feeding frenzy has culminated on more yarn than I can hope to knit in a lifetime.

Don't laugh. I mean every word of it. And I'd like to point out here that I was knitting before it was cool. Before everybody did it and stars showed off their newest circular needles on television. My mother knits, my grandmother knits and my daughters will knit someday. If you could teach pets to do it, Marilyn might be the world's first knitting iguana.

Suz arrives before Sophia, but I expected that. I didn't expect Suz to be carrying two enormous bottles of iced tea and a worried look on her face. Well, I suppose that's a lie. If she'd have left the message to me that I left on her voice mail last night, I'd have shown up expecting disaster, too. Let's just say I was…dazed and confused.

"Sit." Suz shoves the bottle of tea in my lap as we take up residence on the artsy bistro table and chairs Sophia keeps outside her shop. I know these chairs well. Sophia has found me awaiting her arrival on these chairs enough times to offer me a shop key. I don't want it. It'd be like handing candy store keys to a diabetic— some impulses are better off restrained. "Talk," Suz commands.

So I talk. And talk and talk.

I'm just about finished relating the evening's events when Sophia saunters up the street, her giant straw bag once again filled with the most marvelous knitted creations I have ever seen. When I look at Nigel's drawing—even his doodling—I see genius. I see the same genius in Sophia's knitting— even if it's just an ordinary pair of socks.

"Oh," Sophia coos, fishing her keys out of the bag, "that kind of day, is it? I just got some exquisite alpaca in yesterday in those colors you always like." She opens up the shop with a knowing smile, lets us inside, then heads into the back room to settle her belongings. Suz and I begin the comforting ritual of touching everything in sight. Feathery mohairs, perky, bumpy novelty yarns; smooth, stable wools.

"So he was there, huh?" Suz says with her fingers in a ball of red sport yarn. Suz loves red. She's not getting married in February for nothing.

"He's actually been there for the past three years. I just never knew who he was before last night." I pick up a chocolate-brown wool, the color of Kyle's eyes. Kyle has nice eyes.

"You know it's in his professional interest to be nice to you. You know that, don't you?" Suz is staring at me.

"Yes, I know that." Know, agonize over, freak out about; they're all synonyms, right?

Suz's glare goes straight to my stomach. I've told her a dozen times she's already got the eyes to be a great mother—her glare sprouts guilt from twenty yards out. I hide from her in a basket of brightly colored ribbon yarn. "He could be insincere. Ninety percent of the network guys *would* be just kissi—*cozying* up to get on my good side. But he is a Christian, you know. I just want to point that out here. Even if he is a network bad guy, he is a man of faith."

"My," offers Sophia as she pushes aside the curtain from the back room. "Office romance, Lindy dear? That wild Nigel fellow finally tell you how much he likes you?" Sophia has it in her head that Nigel is in love with me and is just too messed up to admit it.

I assure you, Nigel is not in love with me. Nigel and I are purely friends. I know because I've heard all about Nigel's dates, and I am nowhere near what Nigel looks for in a woman. A fact, I must point out here, that gives me great pride. Nigel prefers women with pin-up looks and very few brains. He gets them, too. By the dozens. As Nigel puts it: "Fame's a chick-magnet." Now do you see why I view my office as a mission field?

"And what about Kyle?" Suzann asks.

"Kyle is nice, highly appropriate and very attractive."

So why do I keep thinking about highly inappropriate Leo Corbin?

Sophia comes up, putting a hand on my shoulder. "I always find that when working out an issue of fear, green is best."

"Nope. No green."

Sophia smiles and arranges a container of needles the way other women would arrange a vase of flowers. She's right, you know. My major emotion here is fear. How does she do that? I sit down at the table loaded with pattern books and pretend to leaf through them.

What am I afraid of? Let's see, there's the fear that Kyle likes me only for Maggie Hoot. That's a biggie. Then there's the fear that Leo isn't really as nice as he seems. I should never forget that Leo could take Maggie Hoot away from me. And that's huge. I've spent so much time convincing myself that Maggie Hoot is what I do, not who I am. Suddenly, she's defining my relationships? There isn't enough yarn in California to untangle this.

Suz's voice calls out over a large pile of

mohair skeins. "Do you think this network guy is going to cancel the show?"

Ah, Suz, cutting right to the heart of things. "You know, if I had even a sense of how he was thinking, I'd be a lot calmer. I know he likes the show. He loves the show. But he looks like the kind of guy who wouldn't let that stop him from cancellation. Our ratings haven't been so hot lately."

Sophia starts pulling green and brown yarns out of a bin and matching them up together. She holds a pair of skeins up at me with one eye shut, visually "trying them on" me from across the room like an artist eyeing a subject. "*Arborville*'s ratings have made you nervous before," she says, rejecting the first pair of skeins and digging around the store for a new pair.

"Not this nervous," Suzann offers.

"Everyone's gotten nervous. Lots of shows have gone belly-up within years of winning Emmys. Nigel's even more neurotic than usual. Last week he told me he's thinking of killing off a character at the end of this season."

Suzann stops rummaging and stares straight at me. "Gross. Not you, I hope?"

"I don't think so. I'm pretty sure he'd tell me if it was me."

"He's not going to kill off Maggie," Sophia proclaims without even looking up. "He's too much in love with you."

"You know, Sophia, you seem to know a lot about Nigel for someone who's never even met him." The rust-colored yarn I'm holding would make a fabulous cardigan. I think I'm going to get it.

"I don't need to meet him. It's all in the way he draws Maggie."

This has got to stop. I stare Sophia down. "I am not Maggie Hoot. I merely provide her voice. It's his *job* to draw me—*Maggie* well. Besides, it's not just Nigel—it's Nigel and about two dozen animators in New Zealand. Nigel does not love me."

Sophia starts humming while she digs down to the bottom of a large bin. I catch Suzann's eye, but she merely returns my questioning glare. I am matching up my lovely rust yarn with a pattern when Sophia sings "Here we are!" into the air with a satisfied little melody.

I drop my rust-colored yarn and gasp. It's true, you know, what Sophia says about yarn. It calls to you. Sometimes you go into a store knowing exactly what you're looking for. Most times, though, you don't know what you're looking for until it comes right up and smacks you in the face.

I've been smacked. The yarn in Sophia's hand is lush and deep, oozing softness and comfort. It has just enough fuzziness to make you crave touching it, but not so much you feel like you'll be knitting a Muppet. I want it. I want every skein she's got of it. The undulating waves of color she's holding call to me. They're perfect for the season—the colors look like Spring bursting out of Winter. All greens and blues and creams and browns and…

Oh, no. I said I wouldn't do greens or browns. Especially those greens and browns. They're *exactly* the colors of Leo's and Kyle's eyes. Great. I come in here looking for the knitting project that will help me clear my head, and I end up with *this*.

Of course, Sophia's standing there, smiling, knowing she's now holding a yarn I can't resist. "Exactly what you need, isn't it?"

"Yes," I sigh, walking toward it with my hands held out. It feels every bit as good as it looks. I must have it. Wow, I'm sick, aren't I?

Sophia says it all the time: the yarn *knows*.

Chapter Ten

Thirty seconds and counting...

It's Saturday night, and I am trying not to be disturbed by the fact that the sound system at Kyle's church actually outclasses our studio system. I've just recorded half a dozen audio announcements for Spring Break Bible school.

Not as Maggie Hoot.

They're disappointed.

They did get some Maggie. I am legally able to throw a few of Maggie's catch phrases—which are sort of "public domain"—in her voice, but I must do the text of the announcements as less-exciting

Melinda Edwards, *voice* of Maggie Hoot. Most people just don't understand that I can say Maggie's stuff as Maggie, but not *their* stuff as Maggie. Still, they always want Maggie, and Lindy's a poor substitute. It's why I don't do many personal appearances.

Except for handsome brown-eyed men who are buying me dinner. That doesn't make me shallow, does it?

I tried to get permission to do these announcements in Maggie's voice. Twice. Why? I'm not even sure. Maybe because I shot off my mouth in front of Kyle and told him I was important enough to get clearance from the legal department. Which was boasting, pure and simple. Which is why I'm paying for it now, disappointing Kyle and his sister. I went off, in my flattery-fed frenzy, and hinted at something I had no business offering. Because I wanted Kyle to like me and I thought Maggie was the only way to do it.

Think I'll ever learn?

We pull into the restaurant—which is my favorite, by the way. Points to Kyle for not downgrading once he didn't get his owl. Now it's my turn to grovel. I'm nowhere near as good at it as Kyle was.

"I'm sorry I couldn't be Maggie. I shouldn't have offered in the first place. The legal department obsesses about this kind of stuff. I'd have gotten in a load of trouble."

"S'okay." Kyle says, not quite hiding that it isn't. "It's not like we were paying you or anything."

I hate it when people think I hold back on Maggie for the money. I think it's a stupid rule, too, but contracts are contracts and I want to keep my job. "I'd have done it for free if I could, Kyle. I *did* do it for free, just not as Maggie."

"I know," he replies, smiling a bit. He turns to me, as if suddenly realizing that his last remark was just short of rude. "I'm a jerk when I get around my sister. Thanks for doing it at all—you must get a zillion requests to do this kind of thing. Besides," he says, his smile broadening, "I think Lindy has a pretty cute voice."

"Cuter than Maggie's?" Oh, man, I am shameless.

"Much. Want to reward that mouth for all its hard work?"

For a hormone-crazed second I think he means he's going to kiss me. Which is unwise, unlikely and definitely un-good-girl. Then I come to my senses and realize he means he's going to *feed* me. Can this guy cloud my thinking or what?

The seafood place perches out on a dock, making you feel as if you're dining on a yacht. The sunset is punctuated by swooping pelicans, who hover over the water like stealth aircraft before diving in after their dinner. It's exquisite scenery. Exotic and very romantic—even in January. The low-angled light of the evening sun sets off gold sparks in Kyle's eyes and amber glints in his hair. I sit there, trying not to stare at him, hoping the sunset is doing the same delicious things to my appearance that it's doing to his. I'm startled by how much I want this guy to like me.

"I think we should get the crab," he says. "You can't just get something ordinary like lasagna when we're rewarding you for a job well done."

Well, now, what's one or two dumb comments in the face of an historic fifth date? An *actual* fifth date? With a guy who's told me my voice is cuter than Maggie's? "Much cuter"—you heard those exact words.

We both order the crab, smirking at each other like kids who've just ordered the super-colossal-all-you-can-eat sundae at the ice-cream shop while our parents weren't looking.

"Did I say thanks?" he asks while offering me the bread basket.

"Yes. You're welcome. It was fun." Yes, that's a bit of an exaggeration, but it wasn't nearly as painful as the last *Arborville* taping session so it's not a lie, either.

Kyle leans on one elbow. "It must be so much fun, what you do." He's looking at me like I am the absolute dreamiest thing he's ever seen. I'm liking it.

"Parts of it are. Parts of it are like any other job—boring, tedious, people bickering over tiny details, executives making you do dumb stuff."

"Do you love it?"

You know, no one's ever asked me that before. Everyone always assumes that I love it because who *couldn't* love such a cool job? More points for Kyle. "I've wanted to do this since forever. It really is my dream job. I love even the bad stuff. Sometimes I'm sure they'll pinch me in an hour and I'll wake up from this great dream to discover I'm working behind the counter at a convenience store."

"You're funny," he laughs. After a tiny pause he adds, "How come you were never this funny before?"

Perceptive question. I'm stumped for a moment. "I don't know. Maybe I was trying so hard not to be Maggie that I couldn't be myself. Does that make any sense?"

"I don't know. How could you *not* be Maggie? I mean, she's part of you, you're part of her. She even looks like you—you know that, don't you? Now that I know, I can see it all over the place. The way you cock your head to one side when you make a joke—she does that, too. And your eyes—they have the same look somehow. It's so obvious now that I can't see how I missed it before. I hear it all over your voice, too. Your *normal* voice, that is. Do they look at you when they draw her?"

"Nigel—the creator of the show—knows me really well. He's a good friend, so I suppose he puts some of all of us into our characters. I have had friends say that they can see me in Maggie and Maggie in me. I haven't decided yet whether that's a compliment or just creepy. I mean, she's an owl, not a swan or Miss America or anything."

Kyle flashes the warmest of smiles. "It's a compliment."

I smile back and then hide my blush by taking a long drink of water. For just a moment I let myself take the whole scene in: sunset, adorable guy, impending crab dinner, unprecedented fifth date. Wow. "What do you like about your job?" I ask when I finally recover my composure.

"It's not as cool as yours, that's for sure. When you really get down to it, I just sell office equipment. Very high-tech, very expensive office equipment, but it's just stuff. Still, it's fun—well, maybe satisfying's a better word—to make a really big sale or land a new account." The crab arrives and we both take a moment to savor the fabulous smell. Who knew a man could be so handsome when he inhales?

"The people are nice," Kyle continues. "There's the one office jerk, but every office has to have one, right?"

"I suppose. I always feel like our jerks are more outlandish than your standard-issue sales office jerk. I bet yours don't have as many tattoos."

"Who knows? A button-down shirt can hide a lot. It's not like I ever see the staff in shorts."

Now here is a fine example of just how weird my workplace is. I've seen coworkers in pajamas, in states of undress no other office would ever tolerate, and wearing stuff that would get you fired in any other circumstance. Actually, stuff that would probably get you arrested back in Boston. I'll admit, I dress conservatively by L.A. standards, but I'm no prude. Most of the outlandishness just makes me laugh. Still, I've got my limits. Nigel had a stint of wearing shirts with obscenities on them until I told him I wouldn't stand for it anymore. He thought I was kidding until I brought a pair of pinking shears into work that morning. Applying the broadest Boston accent I could muster from my East Coast heritage, I told him I would shred the next one I found on his person.

Kyle is such a nice dresser. He looks great tonight. Nice looking and wonderfully...*normal*. I am really liking this guy. Do you think he'd wear a scarf if I knit it for him? I've got some yarn in a gold that would set off his eyes....

"Lindy?" Kyle's attempting to regain my attention.

"Oh, sorry. I was just..." I dive in and go for honesty, emboldened by the presence of expensive seafood. "I was just thinking how nice you looked tonight." *Oh, yes, way to go, Lindy! Do you have any idea how stupid that sounded?*

"Funny," he replies, reaching for my hand, "I was just thinking the same thing."

Wow.

The evening flies by so fast it seems like the blink of an eye before Kyle is standing on my apartment steps while I do the fumble-with-my-keys thing. Every single part of this dinner has been perfect. I completely admit it: I am dying for this guy to kiss me. He held my hand through half of dessert and I thought I was going to swoon right off my chair. If he keeps looking at me like that I may just melt on the spot.

In a lush, unhurried movement, Kyle leans in and lets our lips touch. Yes, melt is definitely the right verb here. His hand tightens around mine and pulls me close. It's a tender, soft kiss. Sweet and warm and head-spinning.

After a long moment, he pulls away just enough for our foreheads to touch, his hand still tight on mine. "That was even better than I thought it'd be," he whispers into my hair.

He's thought about kissing me. Double wow.

"I'd better go," he says, sounding as if he'd rather do anything than go right now.

Oh, don't go. Stay right here for the next five years or so. Don't let go of my hand. Don't move an inch.

"No, really." His soft chuckle is like velvet against my cheek. "I think I've got about thirty seconds of good Christian behavior left in me."

Oh, me, too, Kyle.

"I want to see you again, Lindy. I want to see you a lot."

I reach up and push a lock of that dark, glossy hair out of his eyes. "Me, too. I had a really wonderful time."

Kyle reaches up to take that hand, as well, holding both of mine and he takes one step down.

I give in to the silly impulse to blow him a kiss. Okay, it's stupid and sentimental but I am completely smitten at the moment so cut me a break. Kyle winks and gives his car keys a small toss. At first I think he's singing as he rounds the bumper of his car to open the driver-side door.

Then I realize what he's really doing.

"Whoo-whoo. Whoo-whoo."

Kyle is *hooting*.

Chapter Eleven

Walk like an iguana

Suzann is sitting with me in my apartment after church Sunday morning, helping me wind yarn. It works just like in the paintings: one person stands there, holding a loop of yarn between their hands while the other person winds it into balls. Goofy, but totally necessary. Skip this step, and you end up with a ball of tangles and a migraine.

Take this step, and not only do you get orderly yarn, but you get an excellent opportunity to chat with your girlfriend about the disturbing bumper crop of men in your life.

"Is this Leo guy for real?" If Suzann wore

half-moon spectacles, she'd be glaring at me over them. That's the tone of voice she's using. "And if you've kissed Kyle, why are you seeing Leo this afternoon?"

I snip off the yarn and start another ball. "I am not *seeing* Leo. I'm just taking him to meet Marilyn."

Suzann rolls her eyes. "Oh, yes, the lady lizard. Why are you walking her again?"

I admit, not everyone can appreciate Nigel's unique relationship with his iguana. Marilyn may be the closest Nigel ever gets to a committed relationship, so I'm willing to indulge him. "She's had some kind of respiratory thing and she's supposed to get lots of sunlight and socialization. Nigel's in San Francisco for the weekend, so he needs lizard sitters."

"No lizard day care in the yellow pages?" Suzann makes a face.

"Hey, someday I'll be coming over to 'lizard-sit' your little ones and you won't think Aunt Lindy's indulgences are so silly. Which would you rather do? Change a diaper or walk an iguana?"

"That's not even a real question. I don't

have to answer that." You can tell, however, by the dreamy look that comes over Suzann's eyes, that she's already imagined rocking babies to sleep. With her voice, she'll have the calmest infants on the planet. With the greatest hair. She's got all kinds of wedded bliss to look forward to.

Me, I've got scales and rhinestones. Maybe Kyle.

And Leo Corbin.

It's going to be one interesting afternoon.

That afternoon, I stood in Griffith Park, the one outside Nigel's apartment, and asked myself that same question: Why am I walking Marilyn? And why did I invite Leo to come along? I suppose I want to see Leo's reaction to Marilyn. That it will reveal something about his true nature. Animals do that to people. Granted, fuzzy puppies do it better than reptiles, but Marilyn's a special lizard.

Which is why, I suppose, I want to see Marilyn's reaction to Leo. No, I'm not letting a lizard pick my friends for me, I'm just gathering input. Getting a second opinion of sorts. I had a cat back in Boston who could tell a bad guy at twenty paces. Pets know stuff. Right now I need to know everything I can about Leo Corbin.

I'm not quite sure what I expected to happen when I saw Leo again. Especially after last night with Kyle. I think I thought I might find Leo annoying, or at least less attractive. Despite my skepticism, the same zing went through my system when he turned the corner and met me at the park gate. His eyes *are* the exact color green of the yarn back in my apartment. His smile is huge but slightly nervous. Nerves, or effort? Is he as stumped by this attraction as I am? Or just planning the best way to exploit it? I honestly don't have a clue how to proceed here. We fumble out a hello and just stare at each other for a moment.

Suddenly, Leo grabs my hand. "There," he pronounces, "I touched you. You touched me. We got that sticky moment out of the way."

I can't help but laugh. "Do all you executive types tackle problems so…directly?"

"Hey, it took me half an hour to come up with that."

He hasn't let go of my hand. After another long moment, I've got to do something. "So," I blurt out, "if you think you're good with women's hands, this is definitely your day. Marilyn can be a *hand*ful." I admire my witty save if I do say so myself.

"We're really walking an iguana? You weren't kidding?"

"Not at all." I slip my hand out of his to gesture toward Nigel's so-offbeat-it's-trendy town house that's just across the street from the park gate.

"Doesn't Nigel have people to do this?"

"Sure, he has me."

"Not other people? Fans? Minions?"

Well, what do you know? Leo has a small case of lizard nerves. Just wait until he sees how big Marilyn is. Suzann won't even be in the same building as Marilyn, much less take her for a stroll. Me, I find Marilyn fascinating, but I hold a healthy respect for her claws and her prickly personality. "Marilyn's a bit picky about who she likes. I think that's what Nigel likes

most about her. She's rather…demonstra-
tive…about her taste in friends. And she
doesn't like most of Nigel's friends."

"Imagine that." Leo holds the courtyard
gate open for me.

I decide not to reveal that I don't like most
of Nigel's friends, either. "But Marilyn loves
me, and I get a kick out of her." We climb
the short flight of stairs. "By the way," I
advise while opening the first of Nigel's four
door locks, "Nigel's not the neatest of guys.
Even his cleaning lady can't keep up with
him. Just be forewarned."

"Lizard. Slob. Got it."

That proves a smart warning, because
Leo only sucks his breath in a little bit
when we finish lock four and push open
the door to Nigel's town house. He makes
a little whistle as we pick our way through
the clothes, pizza boxes and general
bachelor junk that blocks our way to Marilyn's room.

Yes, Marilyn has a room.

Nigel, because he can and because he
doesn't have enough sense to know any
better, has built Marilyn her own little

habitat in his sunroom. It has everything the modern diva lizard could want—heated rocks, climbing branches, foliage, swimming pools—you name it, Marilyn's got three of them. I unlatch the screen door and invite Leo inside, giving him a moment to take it all in.

Marilyn is, of course, hiding. Waiting, like any good diva, for the proper moment to make her entrance. Leo's rattled, but I remember the first time I met Marilyn. I thought I was going to be eaten alive by a pint-size dinosaur. I give the little whistle Nigel does to call her.

"She comes when called?" Leo whispers to me with a tone of amazement. His head is still craning around to take the whole mini-jungle habitat in.

"Not really. She'll show when she's good and ready." A tail swishes down from a branch just off my left shoulder. "Ah, she must like you to show herself so early. Look over there."

I love to watch people meet Marilyn for the first time. It says so much about them. Will Leo be amazed or freaked? At the moment he looks a little of both; working a bit to stay cool and calm.

"The neat thing about iguanas is that they tell you how they're feeling. Watch her skin. She'll change color as I come closer." I walk toward Marilyn. She swivels her head toward me and turns a lovely combination of lime green and bright orange. I never cease to get a kick out of watching the transformation.

"Whoa!" Leo exclaims quietly from behind me. "Get a load of that! She's a living mood ring."

In that moment, I know Leo gets it. Sure, he's still frightened of her—Marilyn's a big gal who could do serious damage if she chose—but there's that "wow" factor in Leo's voice. I pull Marilyn off her branch and she settles herself on my forearm. She's looking straight at Leo.

Leo points to the rhinestones that stud Marilyn's pink leather harness. "Those aren't…?"

"Swarovski crystals, not diamonds. Nigel's bad, but not that bad." Marilyn looks straight at Leo and turns bright green.

"Hey, that's iguana for 'I like you.'" She moves down my arm closer toward Leo, who seems determined not to flinch. "Seems you're a hit."

"As long as I'm not a bite, I'm okay with that."

I take Leo's hand and guide it to the back of Marilyn's neck. "If you stroke her here, she'll be your best friend." He does, and Marilyn arches her head up and closes her eyes luxuriously. Honestly, she looks like a woman getting a foot massage—she's got that "ooo, yes, right there" look on her face.

"She's amazing," he says. He's standing awfully close to me.

Flustered, I gather up Marilyn's leash and we head out into Griffith Park. People stare. They always stare. It's hard to be discreet with a little Godzilla on your shoulder. Just as we get to a nice sunny patch of grass, Marilyn decides Leo would make better furniture. In two quick movements, she climbs off me and makes a little jump onto Leo's shoulder.

You can't really blame the guy for yelping. Marilyn's got a set of nails Cruella DeVille would envy, and he had no forewarning. "Um," Leo says, trying to force control back into his voice, "what color is she now?"

"Oh," I reply, reminding myself it would be cruel to laugh, "she's a very friendly shade of green. You've got a new admirer."

"You got any iguana treats or lizard chow or whatever? I'd like to cement the friendship before she wraps her tail around my neck or something." He's almost laughing, but still a little too scared to find the situation funny.

I hand him a little tin of treats and settle back to watch the show of Leo making friends with Marilyn. He's talking to her, stroking her—

Ahem. Leo's making friends with Marilyn. Let's just leave it at that.

Finally, after a bizarre version of "keep away" where Marilyn darted between Leo and I as we tossed treats back and forth— all part of "socialization and exercise"— our emerald-colored charge spreads herself out on the grass to soak up some sun.

Leo tucks his hands behind his head and lays back on the grass. I wrap the end of

Marilyn's leash around my hands and lay back on my side, propped up on one elbow. I still can't read this guy and it bothers me. Is he genuinely nice, or just very good at what he does?

"Did you have pets growing up?" he asks.

"Nothing this exotic. A short-lived goldfish I won in the sixth-grade carnival. A dog. A hamster. The usual stuff. What about you?"

"I grew up in the country, so we had lots of animals. A bunch of dogs, cats in the barn, even horses. Let's just say I got my start a far cry from L.A."

"So how'd you end up here?"

"Iron will. I was so eager to get out of Hicksville and make my name in the industry that I would have crawled over broken glass to get here. I made sure I landed the best internship out of college and worked my backside off until they noticed me. Been working it off ever since."

"They noticed you, trust me. I looked you up on Google, and people either love you or hate you, but they definitely notice you." It's out of my mouth before I even realize I've made the embarrassing admission that I researched the guy. Why don't I just get a marker and write Control Freak across my forehead?

"You looked me up on the Internet?" Leo cranes one eye open to look at me. "I'm flattered—I think. Can I assume—" he comes up on one elbow, as well, so we're lying face-to-face "—that since you're still speaking to me, I didn't come up completely repulsive? I mean, for an evil network spy and all?"

His expression is…roguish. Yes, "roguish" really *is* the word. I know it's sort of a *Jane-Eyre*-esque vocabulary, but the guy has a civilized-yet-playful air about him. As if you're nervous about what he'll do next, but you want to be around for it anyway.

"Hey, this is TV land. Everyone looks up everyone on Google." In my wild attempt to cover up my own compulsive behavior, I hit on the perfect strategy. "Fess up, you checked me out on Google, didn't you?"

He's blushing. Did you see that? Leo Corbin is actually blushing.

"That's different," he defends. "I have

to. Professional research." I eye him. Leo throws his hands up in defeat and falls back onto the grass. "But, yeah, I'd have done it anyway."

After a moment, he rolls his head over to look at me. "Still," he says with a disarming tone in his voice, "you have way more hits than me."

"That's different." I lie back in the grass, as well, half to cross my arms over my chest and half to keep Leo's eyes from yanking down my defenses. I apply my best diva face while squinting my eyes shut against the sun. "I'm *supposed* to be famous."

"And I'm supposed to not let my personal feelings get in the way of my work."

Oh my. He's looking right at me, I can feel it. Leaning toward me, maybe. We have officially achieved "complicated." I'm terrified to open my eyes.

Suddenly, I hear Leo yelp and feel a surging force pulling my right hand off my arm. Leo was, in fact, leaning closer to me, but evidently sank a knee into Marilyn's tail in the process. She's letting her displeasure be known by scrambling to get away from the two of us—mostly right over Leo's legs. "Ow! Get her off me!"

Leo and I sit bolt upright to find a bright turquoise lizard in the process of shredding Leo's jeans. Turquoise, of course, being lizard for "Ouch, you incompetent minions who were supposed to be watching me!"

"Well," I offer, rubbing my wrist and reaching for Marilyn, who eyes me with a soundly annoyed expression, "I was thinking it'd be an interesting afternoon."

Leo, on the other hand, is rubbing his shin and wincing. There are several nasty tears in the leg of his jeans. "Oh, memorable, that's for sure."

Chapter Twelve

Monday, Monday

When you begin knitting a multicolored yarn, one color invariably dominates the piece. You never know which color it will be. You've got to just start knitting and see what the yarn chooses to be.

Catch the metaphor here?

After that major moment in college when all those voices jumped out of my mouth, I knit like a fiend for months. I was so broadsided by the sudden overwhelming desire to ditch journalism and go into entertainment, I looked anywhere for guidance. Including yarn colors.

It didn't work any better then than it does now. The hard truth was that no one could tell me which choice was best. It was a decision only I and God could make, and every logical evaluation, every career guidance test, even every shred of friendly advice didn't really help.

I knit anyway. If nothing else, it kept me busy until my soul sorted things out.

I got a lot of knitting done after that day with Leo. Row after row, I kept waiting again for the yarn to offer me up some kind of message. More brown or more green? Kyle or Leo?

Of course, no hint came. It was late into the night before I finally wised up and remembered again that prayer was probably a better coping strategy than needlework.

Still no clarity. By the time I slunk off to bed, I couldn't tell you who was winning: the side of me that wanted to kiss Marilyn for saving me from getting caught up in Leo's charm, or the side of me that was ready to ship the shredding little beast off to Prada to become a handbag.

Ah, the joys of Monday on nowhere
near enough sleep.

As I said earlier, Mondays are usually the
best days around Treehouse. We do the table
read and laugh because it's always so good.

Today, I'm in no mood to laugh. I'm so
tired and confused that I'm ready to call in
sick. We have a guest voice on the show
this week, though, and I can't bring myself
to do anything so unprofessional.

The script usually arrives in the middle
of the night via messenger. Nigel and his
writing team are always tinkering with it
right up until the last minute, especially
when we have a high-profile guest on the
show. Early on, I would stay up and wait
for it. Last night I'm sure I was awake long
enough to hear it thunk through the mail
slot I had to have built into my door for just
such deliveries. These days I simply grab
it on my way out the door, flipping through
it at stoplights if I feel like it. Today, I only
flipped through it enough to learn who our
guest voice would be.

I should have left it unread. This would be
a nice week for Mel Gibson or Heath Ledger

or Pierce Brosnan—you know, someone with a sparkling personality and a distracting set of...vocal cords. But oh, no, this week we get Axe Martin, aging heavy metal rock-n-roll icon. Aren't you thrilled?

Every once in a while, Nigel goes for pure shock value in a guest voice. Axe is pure shock. Axe is pure trouble, too. How do I know, you ask? I know because "his people" arrive before he does. Let me introduce you to a phenomenon known as the Hollywood entourage. There they are—intense young men in expensive suits, unnaturally clean sneakers and hundred-dollar sunglasses. They swoop in here like the Secret Service, barking orders into their cell phones and whipping out their PDAs. They always spell trouble.

Leo's somewhere in the building, too. I know he is. Still, I've wimped out and tried to avoid him. I know he'll be at the table read, but he'll be in full-blown executive mode and I'm not ready to see that. I keep my coffee cup full and my head down as we gather around the giant conference table where the reads take place. Occasionally, we have a small audience of VIPs who sit in the ring of chairs that lines the room walls—attending an *Arborville* table read is a hot ticket, especially with a guest. It's standing room only this morning.

The room is buzzing as we pass around the show merchandise we need to autograph this week. Animation cells, stuffed dolls, plastic figures, T-shirts. Animation is the only industry where you know you've made it when tiny plastic yous end up in paper sacks with cheeseburgers and French fries. This is the time I most feel like a celebrity. I know it's a picture of Maggie and not of me, but it still feels like the coolest job on the planet when I remember that many of these things are heading to charity auctions, children's hospitals, stuff like that. I look up, just as I finish the last signature, to see Leo secure a spot in the corner. My pulse does a hop, and I am glad he's not looking in my direction—I definitely do not want to meet those eyes right now.

I'll give Axe Martin one thing: he showed up. Not every guest does. Some just blow in for the tapings, insist on as few takes as possible, and blow out again back to their movie sets or concert tours. I'm trying to do the Christian thing here, and not prejudge Mr. Martin. He might be a really nice guy, despite the conspicuous advance team. The dark eyeliner and head-to-toe leather might just be a stage persona.

No such luck. Here he comes. How do you guess he sits in those pants? They can't be comfortable; they're seventy per cent metal studs. I can see enough of the writing on his T-shirt to know I'm glad his leather jacket is hiding the rest. I have never understood how balding men can think the remaining hair should be grown long enough for a ponytail. Looking at his face, you can see he was a dangerous brand of handsome in his youth. The stuff of high school bedroom posters. The definitive bad boy. Hang on to your scripts, folks, it's going to be a wild morning.

"Can you *believe* he did that?" Kelly Alberts, the voice of Lillith Robin, is gawking at me over post-table-read coffee.

"I think he swore every other word," I reply. It really was an awful morning. The script was definitely not one of Nigel's best. It had a weird sense of desperation to it—but maybe I'm picking up on something that's not there thanks to my own disorientation. Martin was every inch the foulmouthed rock star. I even think he may have had a bit more than coffee to drink this morning. Or maybe he's just not a morning person, being a rock star and all. I'm trying to be nice here.

"No," says Kelly, evidently unfazed by Martin's language, "I mean the script. Why did Nigel do that?"

I sigh. "Why does Nigel do anything?"

"A serial killer? *Arborville* needs a serial killer?"

"He wasn't really one in the end. That's the whole point." I start pouring another cup of coffee, but stop myself; a sixth would be crazy. I'll be awake till next season if I have any more caffeine.

"Still," says Kelly, sorting through her mail as she stands at the coffee-room counter. "He was just creepy. The guy, I

mean. And his character was just creepier."
Kelly was once a flight attendant, runner up
for Miss North Dakota and voices several
fluffy Saturday-morning cartoon characters. Get the picture?

"Well, you can hardly call in somebody cute and cuddly to play that type of
character. He was playing a vampire bat,
after all. His voice works because everyone knows who he is and what he is."

Kelly narrows her eyes. "I'll tell you
what he is…"

"Can we talk about something else?"
I'm in no mood to defend Nigel or trash
Axe Martin's personal integrity.

Kelly shoots me a look. "Suit yourself.
Hey, speaking of suits, our resident
network spy is over talking to Osgood right
now. With the *door shut.*"

Evan Osgood is our executive producer.
The only person who outranks Nigel—and
just barely at that. He's a tall, lanky guy
who spends his life worrying. Why?
Because Osgood is supposed to keep Nigel
in line. There isn't enough money in the
world to make me take that job. Nigel

doesn't do "in line." I'm not even sure Nigel knows there *is* a line.

So Leo's talking to Osgood. Behind closed doors. This is the definition of "not good." I'm getting that sixth cup of coffee—I'll be up all night worrying anyway.

I push open my office door, juggling papers and coffee, to find Nigel sitting cross-legged on top of my desk.

Next to a large vase of flowers.

"Well, doll, seems you did more than just watch my lizard this weekend. Who's Kyle?"

"*Nice* people," I say, snatching the card out of Nigel's hand, "do not read other people's mail. Off!"

"Aw, love," Nigel pouts and leaps off my desk like a rumpled puppy. "When have I ever been nice?"

I glare at Nigel and read the card:

Owl be seeing you again this weekend I hope? Say yes.
—Kyle

"'Owl be seeing you.' Couldn't you just *die?*" Nigel swoons against my credenza.

Like I said, there are days I yearn to work with accountants. Or shoe salesmen. Normal people.

"Don't you have to go be brilliant somewhere?"

"I've got a meeting in twenty minutes, but until then, I'm all yours." He drapes himself over my office chair. "Didn't you love the script this morning? It's right up your thematic alley; 'judge not, lest ye be judged' and all."

I should be thankful Nigel can recite a Bible verse. It means he may have actually read the five or six Bibles I've given him over the years. Today, though, I'm in no mood for Nigel's theatrics—on or off the page. "That wasn't one of your best and you know it. Don't let Corbin spook you into doing something stupid just to boost ratings. You're better than that. And look at you—how hard did you party it up in San Francisco? I'm not going to watch your lizard just so you can poison yourself in another zip code."

Just in case you haven't figured it out

yet, Nigel has a bit of a substance problem. He'd been doing really well until all this ratings mess turned up the pressure. I wouldn't call him an addict, just someone who doesn't know the meaning of moderation in anything. Work, food, money, publicity—it's "everything all the time" in Nigel's world.

"So who's Kyle?" says Nigel, determined to change the subject. "Same bloke you went to dinner with last week?" He's snapped a flower off my bouquet and is using my tape to stick it to the lapel of his leather coat. It makes him look like a punked-out Charlie Chaplin.

Some days Nigel is so far over the top that he just makes my heart ache. *Lord, couldn't You just get through to him for ten seconds? He's a disaster waiting to happen if You don't save him.*

"I like Kyle," I reply as I snatch my tape back, tucking it in my top drawer. Why are men always taking things off my desk? "He likes me. We talk, we eat dinner, we do things together. It's called a relationship. You should try it some time."

"This the same mate who freaked out about Maggie?"

Remind me to never discuss my so-called love life with you, no matter how many bags of cheese curls you buy me. "Well, he was a little weird about it at first, but," and I emphasize the next point by looking straight into Nigel's bloodshot eyes, "lots of people in my life are weird."

"Want to invite him to next week's reading so we can all meet him? I've got a fab script in the hopper. Brilliant. Emmy material."

"No." As if I'd ever let anyone meet this bunch before the twentieth date. No thank you.

Suddenly I hear Leo's voice coming down the hallway. Eek, I'm not ready to see him. Not with Nigel draped across my chair, waving his arms and legs like a beetle stuck on its back. "Does anybody know where—" he stops in my doorway "—Nigel is?"

"Yoo-hoo! Here I am, Mr. Network Nasty." Nigel calls out in such a melodramatic, mean-spirited way that I am embarrassed for him. Nigel's never been professional, but right now he's behaving like a complete fool. I don't want him endangering the show by antagonizing Leo or doing something else just as destructive.

Leo stands in the doorway, his face mirroring the near disgust I am feeling. His gaze starts on Nigel, finds its way to me for a moment, then finally rests on the huge bouquet of flowers to my left. He straightens. His face becomes expressionless, unreadable.

When he finally speaks, Leo's voice is all business. "Osgood would like to see you, if you have a moment." Can everyone else see that Leo's gaze has not left the flowers, or is it just me?

"Well, now, can't keep Mr. Osgood waiting, can we? I'm off. Lindy, love, why don't you spend a few moments convincing Mr. Network why we're such a friend of the empire. Everybody just *loves* Maggie Hoot, don't they?"

It's official: I want to die.

Chapter Thirteen

Do not panic until instructed to do so

"Is he always like that?"

I am completely unready to deal with Leo in a business setting. My brain is working overtime to try and mesh the Leo I met this weekend with the Leo in front of me. I messed up four lines of dialogue during the table read.

"No," I reply. "I mean not *that* bad. *You* make him that bad. Congratulations, you're taking Nigel right over the edge. It won't be pretty, I assure you."

"'Me' as in the evil minion of the network me, or my own individual sparkling demeanor?"

Oh, now, there's the question of the hour. Which one of you is it that freaks Nigel out? For that matter, which one of you is it that freaks me out? Bing! Survey says: both!

"Letter c: all of the above."

Leo, still standing in the doorway, glances left and right as if checking for eavesdroppers. Evidently finding none, he takes a step inside; he parks one hip on my credenza and stares at me. "I…um…don't know how to do this."

He's going to tell me he's axing the show. I just know it. That's why he was with Osgood. This morning's script wasn't good enough. It hasn't even been the five weeks and he's decided we're not worth saving. "Do…what?" I stammer out.

Leo's glance sweeps around the room. "This. Here." Then, very quietly, he adds, "Us."

My whole body reacts to that. He's not axing the show. There's an "us"? One whopping load of impact for three little words, don't you think? "Aren't you moving a bit fast? Shouldn't we just try and behave normally? Do the show stuff at the show, and do the other stuff…if there even is other stuff to do…away from the office." I'm cringing. That was the most cumbersome sentence ever strung together. What is it with this guy and my instant loss of communication skills?

"Yeah, good idea." Leo doesn't seem any more articulate in my presence than I am in his. "Yep," he repeats, twirling his pen.

I can't stand it. "Okay," I pronounce, leaning back on my chair so as to appear in control—note the use of the word *appear.* "So, what would you be asking me right now if we hadn't been recently escorting an angry iguana?" *Ooo, that was commanding and clever. Score one for Lindy.*

"What did you think of the script?"

Nope, I definitely do not like the way he said that. Perhaps this was the wrong tactic. Behave normally. Do not panic until instructed to do so. Answer him just as you would have one week ago.

"Not Nigel's best. You guys breathing down his back make him go for shock value that didn't need to be there. I'll bet the first draft of the script—the one Nigel and the writing team cooked up before you got here—is much better." The sudden need to defend *Arborville* surges up inside me. "Nigel's brilliant. He's brilliant without trying. It's when you guys make him think he has to try harder that things get out of whack."

"Who sent the flowers?"

"What?" Talk about your whiplash-inducing change of subject.

"Is it your birthday or something? Who sent the flowers?"

"Hey, I thought we were trying to act normal here." I do not want to answer this question.

"I'd probably have asked under normal conditions."

"Not with *that* look on your face, you wouldn't. I thought we were talking about the script." Feeling suddenly brave—or maybe just desperate—I opt for a subject change of my own. "And what were you doing in Osgood's office?"

"No, it's not your birthday. They'd have

sung or had cake or something at the read-through. Who sent the flowers?"

"Come on," I counter, somehow feeling a bit invaded, "We're professional talent here, not kindergartners. It's not like we all have our moms bring in treats on our birthday. What'd you say to Osgood?" This has now become a verbal sparring match, each with a secret the other wants to know.

"Who sent 'em? A guy?"

Oh, man, I do not want to get into this. But, oh, man, I need to know what Leo's saying to Osgood. "Well, yes." I measure my words carefully. "The sending party did *happen* to be male."

"Male as in 'hey, I admire your work' male, or male as in 'when can I see you again' male?" Leo is staring hard at the flowers, as if the petals contain clues to the sender's motive.

I'm suspecting Leo of getting far too nosy, until I remember I told him on Friday at the animation festival that I had a date Saturday night. "That's more than one question. First, you tell me what you talked about with Osgood."

Leo, sensing he's been temporarily out-maneuvered, crosses his hands over his chest. "We talked about the writing staff. I asked him how he'd feel about being less dependent upon Nigel."

I had thought of this in terms of two choices: ax the show or not. Never did I ever consider the option that Leo might recommend to ax Nigel. Nigel is *Arborville*'s creator. You don't fire creators. Nigel is *Arborville* and *Arborville* needs Nigel. What if Leo doesn't think so? In a single, sinking moment, I realize I'm going to have to reveal more about the flowers if I'm going to learn more about Leo's conversation. I've not outwitted anyone.

"They're from the man I had dinner with Saturday night." Then, in a burst of brilliance, I add, "I recorded some promo spots for his church's Spring Break Bible school." Mind you, I have not lied. Those two facts are true. They're just not related. You know that, and I know that, but Leo doesn't know that. "Exactly *what* about depending less on Nigel?"

"Expanding the writing team is just one

of several options we have. I'm not recommending we do anything like that. I'm not recommending anything right now, Lindy. It's my job to think through all possibilities, remember?"

"Do you always think through possibilities with the door shut?" It came out more sharply than I would have liked.

"How many people do you have watching me?" There's an edge to his voice, as well.

"I don't have anyone watching you. People are panicking very nicely on their own with no help from me. We're not fools. You go into Osgood's office and shut the door, it doesn't take Einstein to figure out something serious is going on."

Leo takes a step forward and brings his voice down. "You'd prefer I air my concerns about Nigel in the coffee room? I know my presence sets the rumor mill into high gear. I'm trying to maintain a little professionalism here."

"Yeah, by asking me about my floral status. That's integrity."

"Would you be asking me about Osgood if I were anybody else?"

"I don't know." I can't believe I practically shouted that. "Would you be telling me if I were anybody else?"

Leo thrusts one hand into his pocket. "Don't get like this, Lindy."

"I'm not getting like anything. You came into my office, remember? I was just sitting here—"

"Amid a huge bouquet of flowers…."

"Sitting here," I grind out through my teeth because men are such pride-soaked territorial Neanderthals, *"trying* to do my job in spite of lunatic writers and nosy networks." I grab my handbag out of the desk drawer. "Actually, I *don't* have to sit here and try to do my job, my job is done." I stuff a handful of files into a tote bag. "I did my job today, and I can go home now. Tell me, Leo, should I be updating my demo tape in my spare time?"

Leo's pacing my tiny floor now. For once I see the guy truly angry. It's scary. He looks every bit the network axman, like someone who eats failing shows for lunch. We're doomed.

"For once and for all, Lindy, I am not here to oversee the end of your career."

"Prove it!" *Okay, wait, I didn't mean that. Do over. Strike that from the record. Take two....*

Leo reaches over one long arm and slams my door shut so hard that papers fly off my credenza. He stalks over to the desk and plants both hands on it, glaring.

"I do *not* want to cancel *Arborville*. I like the show. I want it to go on. I am not the enemy here." I fight the urge to sink back in my chair, away from the intensity in his eyes. "If you want to know who is *Arborville*'s worst enemy, it's Nigel. He's his own worst enemy. I think you know that. If this show goes down, it'll be because Nigel brings it down around himself. You and I both know this morning's script was way off—you said so yourself."

He pushes himself up off the table and I feel myself exhale the breath I didn't even know I was holding. Leo's walking toward the door. This is the wrong way to leave things. "Leo…"

His hand is on the doorknob. I can't think of anything to say.

"I'm jealous. Are you happy?" Leo says it in a staccato tone, without turning around. "You had a date Saturday night and you've got flowers and I didn't send them and I'm jealous. And I shot off my mouth because…because I haven't the slightest idea how to deal with you and it makes me crazy."

That's either the biggest risk of truth, or the smoothest line ever. I want to believe it, but I'm not sure I can. My life is spinning out of control right in front of my face. I can't bring myself to say anything. I sit there, torn, still clutching my files and staring at his back. He has not moved. Not one inch.

"Save us, Leo." It gulps out of my mouth before I can think.

"I'm trying."

Chapter Fourteen

You know what they say...

"As ye knit, so shall ye rip."

That's a sign that hangs in Fiber Content. It's all too true. I've ripped out far more than I've knitted in the last three hours.

I hightailed it out of the studio shortly after my conversation—if you can call that a conversation—with Leo. Most days I hang around long after the table read, chatting with people, making jokes, churning through piddly office details and generally hanging out.

Today I couldn't get out of there fast enough. Today I wanted to crawl up onto my couch with my knitting and tell the world to get lost. That is, I suppose, one of the better things about my job—with certain ironclad exceptions, I control my own hours. Sure, I've got to drag myself into tapings whether I feel like I'm going to be sick in between takes or not, but nobody needs me to punch a clock otherwise. Monday being the day off for most of the theater community, I could call a few actor friends, but I don't really feel like talking to *anyone*. I put the radio on because Suz is on the air right now, but turned it off after a few minutes. I really don't want to be with any member of the human race right now. Maybe I should get a cat. Or cashmere goats—that would cut down on my yarn bill.

Or just get some results. Which, on this particular sweater, are not happening. I keep messing up the stitch pattern and ending up with holes where they shouldn't be, and bumps where holes should be. Part of my problem might be the scenery. I'm sitting on my couch with my lovely flowers from Kyle on one end of the coffee table, and that troublesome script from *Arborville* on the other.

Lord, my heart groans, *what's going on? I had a great life, a great job and no dates. Now I have a stress-filled life, my job is looking worse every minute and let's not even start in on the men. I want to trust You with all this, but I'm so stressed out I'm clutching at everything. Can I have a hint at what's going on? Some sense of where all this chaos is heading? Or, at least, some inner peace to cope with it all?*

I look down to see I've dropped two stitches. *Sigh.* Unraveling. Yep, that's what it feels as if my life is doing. Unraveling right before my eyes.

Then there's Kyle. Attractive, attentive, non-conflict-of-interest Kyle. Do you think he picked those flowers out himself or did he order them online? Think of him standing there, describing me to the florist, saying, "do you think she'd like these?" I imagine the knowing smile on the florist's face, watching Kyle's nervous choices, ranking Kyle amongst all the other love-struck young men she's served over the years. I'll bet she suggested the apricot roses.

I pick the card up again, to look at Kyle's handwriting.

Petals.com. And it's typed.

Well, it's the thought that counts, right?

Sigh. Knit three, pearl two, yarn over… oh, *drat.* Where do those bumps keep coming from? I rip out that last row and try again. It still doesn't look right. I am ready to throw the whole thing across the room, hoping my needles embed themselves in the far wall, when the phone rings.

Just watch, I smirk to myself. *It'll be one of them.* I have got to get that caller ID thing fixed on my phone.

"Hullo, love."

It's Nigel. *Lovely.*

"What now, Nigel?" I moan, hoping somehow he might actually read my annoyance between the lines.

"You left." And I called this guy brilliant.

"Yes." Nothing says "I don't want to talk to you right now" like monosyllabic answers, right?

"You okay, love?"

"Fine." Silence. "Nigel, is there some *reason* why you called?"

"No, just wanted to check in."

"Okay, well, thanks, I'm fine. I just wanted to get some knitting done." *How lame does that sound? How much lamer is it that it's true?*

"Sure? You botched loads of dialogue this morning. You sick?"

Of your antics, yes. "I'm fine, Nigel. I'll nail it at the taping, I always do." The control freak in me is already crazy about my bad performance this morning, I don't need Nigel turning me up two notches.

"Sure?"

"*Goodbye,* Nigel."

"All right then. Off I go."

"Off you go." I hang up before Nigel can think of something else to say. Experience teaches me not to let go of the phone just yet. Nigel has yet to have any conversation with me in just one phone call. Do you think Jesus will give me bad points on mercy if I let the machine pick up?

Sixty seconds later, the phone rings.

"What now, Nigel?"

"Lindy?"

It's Kyle. The first guy to send me flowers in who knows how long, and I start off using another guy's name. Nice.

"I'm sorry, Kyle, I've been fielding calls from our creator all morning."

"Our Creator? You get phone calls from *God?* You *are* important!" Kyle quips.

"Very funny. Creator with a small *c*. As in Nigel Langdon, head lunatic at Tree-house Studios."

"Big day at work?"

"Just a bit stressful. My desk, however, had never looked better, thanks to you. Now my coffee table's queen of the living room. They're lovely."

"Glad you liked them. Speaking of being liked, my niece and sister went on and on to everyone at church yesterday about how great the announcements are. When they play them next week, you'll be a huge hit."

I'm grinning at how much he's enjoying this. "It was fun. Your equipment's top-notch. That system could make anyone sound good." It's true. Even Elmo could sound commanding on the audio toys they've got over there.

"Dinner was nice, too. I had a great time."

Dinner really was nice. And delightfully uncomplicated. When I hear the cool, smooth tones of Kyle's voice—even though I know part of it is the intrinsic hush of a personal call made from work—I tingle. I think of the sunset pouring gold light into his hair, and my stress starts to dissolve. Am I ready to see Kyle again? You betcha. "Dinner was wonderful," I reply.

"My sister's having a party this weekend. A casual thing, mostly for church people. As a matter of fact, lots of people who work on the Spring Break Bible school will be there. Will you come with me?"

Dinner with the family? Whoa, am I ready for that? Oh, wait, I've already met his sister, so it's not as if he's taking me home to meet his folks or anything. He's just showing me around his world. I like that.

"I'd love to. Can I bring anything?"

"Just your voice. And the pretty package it comes in."

That was a compliment, wasn't it? Okay,

Longfellow he's not. But he sent flowers and he's not arguing with me or slamming my office door. "We'll both be there."

"Fabulous. Got a meeting in ten minutes—I gotta go. I'll be watching you, though."

Huh? Somebody got a telescope I'm not aware of? "What?"

"Tomorrow night. I'll be watching you on TV."

"Oh, right." It's so much of a given that my friends watch the show, I'm always a little tripped up when somebody new thinks to mention it. "Well, we love it when you do." *Tell all your friends. Our ratings can use every ally we can find.*

"Catch you later, Lindy." His voice has an eagerness to it that makes me want to start humming.

"See you, Kyle. And thanks for the flowers."

I am still smiling when I decide to return to my knitting. I try a few rows. Aha! This time it actually *works*. No angry bumps. And the lacy little holes are right where they should be. The sweater of my dreams taking shape in my artful little hands.

And what do you know? That yarn is far more brown than it is green.

You know what they say; *the yarn knows....*

Chapter Fifteen

Poorly drawn smiley faces

The week goes much more quickly than I would have imagined. Especially under the circumstances. Leo vanishes back to the network for a few days. I decide to keep a low profile, coming in only when I need to and offering to help Suz with wedding tasks in my expanded free time. If there was ever a week where falling behind in my correspondence was worth it, this is it.

The one thing that *is* working harder than ever, however, is the rumor mill. There's talk that Jason is leaving the show. I don't set much stock in this because

Jason has started that rumor before. Usually when he's miffed at Nigel or thinks he's not getting enough screen time.

There's another rumor that we'll be moved to one of those death-knell time slots—one opposite a huge hit on another network—to ensure this will be our final season. I count on my fingers, trying to calculate the number of shows we have in production—we're only a few scripts away from having the entire season all set. Until I remember one very important fact: having a show in the can does not necessarily mean it will see the light of day.

Lord, I beg you, I'm too young to be a has-been.

That became my nonstop prayer when Thursday's taping rolled around and Axe Martin looked even older than he did on Monday. I watch the way people vacillate between being impressed at what he once was and looking at him with pity for what he is now, and my fear level rises. Axe is still trying to recapture his moment in the sun. Am I living the sunset of mine?

"C'mon, ducks, get your heads in the

right places!" Nigel barks into everyone's headphones during one nasty taping session. Jason's tried ad-libbing, thinking somehow we will all discover his heretofore unknown brilliance, and the results have been disastrous. That's making Nigel mad enough, but Axe seems to think it's funny, so he keeps snickering over other people's dialogue. Kelly is starting to look slightly alarmed; she's been picking at the rim of her foam coffee cup so that it looks as though a small snowstorm has erupted around her designer shoes.

And me? I've blown my lines. Three times.

Everybody else is acting unprofessionally, and that's bad enough, but now I'm making far too many mistakes. I'm thinking they don't make a banana shake big enough to get me over this disaster.

"All right, kiddies," Nigel finally bellows from the control booth. "We're wasting everyone's money. Take five minutes, find your heads wherever they wandered off to, and come back. Axe, they tell me you've got time so let's give ourselves a break and come back to it fresh, eh?"

Jason rolls his eyes, applying an expression designed to let us all know he feels he's working far below his talent level. Axe seems a bit stupefied that this stuff is as hard as it is, and is trying not to look as if he's working too hard at it. Kelly looks as if she might actually cry if this goes on much longer. None of this is new. We've had bad tapings before. Not quite as bad as this, but bad enough.

The one expression I really can't endure right now is Leo's. He's standing at the back of the control booth, that eternal clipboard in his hand, looking as if he's watching a car crash. Or a stand-up comic bomb on stage. Or the contestants' sad, bitter speeches after being booted off the *Survivor* island. Something pitiful but riveting.

This, you understand by now, is not the reaction you want to see in your friendly neighborhood network executive.

When break's over, Nigel implements an excellent idea. We'll tape our lines individually. From a technical standpoint, it's actually easier. Many shows always do it that way. You do lose some of the banter you might get between actors playing off each other—which can often be fabulous. There are times, though, when it's the best approach. Times like this morning, when catastrophe seems to be contagious. Lucky me, I get to go last. Good thing I brought my knitting.

"Okay, love," Nigel starts as I finally settle into the sound booth and slide my earphones on. "Give me perfection like you always do. And play that last line out real slow—it'll work with what Axe has given us."

I trip over my first line. I'm spooked by what happened earlier. I'm spooked by what's happened all week. I'm spooked by the fact that Leo seems to be scribbling furiously in the control booth behind Nigel.

"Once more, love. Just relax."

I mispronounce Axe's character's name on my second line. Nigel says nothing, but I can see his body language through the glass—shoulders slumping, shaggy head shaking back and forth. He's swearing in there, I just know it.

Suddenly, I catch sight of it: Leo is holding up his clipboard so I can see it, with the word *MILK SHAKE?* in large block letters. I can't help but smile. Before I can even think of a discreet way to reply, he whips the first page off to reveal a second, which reads *REALLY B-I-G MILK SHAKE!* with the most poorly drawn smiley face I have ever seen.

I burst out laughing so hard I whack my head against the microphone, sending a loud *boom* into Nigel's ears and causing the technician to have to come back in and reposition the mike. Nigel is looking around the control booth, saying "What? What?" but no one seems to have noticed the source of my giggle fit because Leo was behind everyone else, and he's somehow managed to hide the makeshift cue cards.

The scene—Nigel looking around, technicians scrambling, Leo trying to keep a straight face—plays out like a silent film through the glass in front of me. It is just too funny.

Once I can finally catch my breath, I deliver every piece of dialogue in one take.

* * *

"I suppose I should say thanks," I admit, straw in hand, as we sit in my favorite booth at Hogan's. This time I ordered the large, with real ice cream, not frozen yogurt. Don't give me any speeches about using food as comfort—I know full well what dietary havoc I'm wreaking. "How did you know it would work?" I ask.

"In my field, you make a lot of people nervous. I've gotten good at breaking the ice. Never quite held a sign up in a taping session before, though. And the thought of drawing *anything* in front of Nigel Langdon made me tense up."

I giggle. "It showed. Your smiley face guy looked like he'd suffered a stroke."

"Ow, that's harsh." Leo makes a pained gesture but he's laughing, too. "I had to do something, and I didn't have a lot of options. You have to remember I just sat through Jason's twelve takes."

"'Raw data,' remember? You sat through the entire taping session last week."

"That was last week. This week I know everyone a bit better, so I don't really need forty minutes of Jason's grandstanding. Not a subtle guy, that Jason."

"He's the favorite character on the show. He's got leverage. He doesn't need charm."

"Mr. Martin, however, could use a little charm. And a better vocabulary. Between him and Nigel, we were clocking a dozen obscenities a minute. Thankfully not in the parts we were taping. How do you stand it every week?"

"Luckily," I say after a huge gulp that slides down my throat like liquid grace, "I don't have to deal with an Axe every week. And Nigel isn't always that bad. He has such a big heart behind all that messed-up life that I can't help but keep pulling for him. Nigel's a project of sorts. If Jesus ever finally gets through to him, he'll turn the world upside down. He'll reach people no one's ever reached before. I guess I'm just hanging on until that happens."

Leo looks thoughtful. "Do you think it will ever happen?"

"God only knows—literally. There are times when he asks really deep questions, and I think there's light shining through. Then he goes off and does something dumb or outrageous or…I don't know—pick your vice, Nigel's probably done it. And then, I don't know. I suppose I'm hoping Jesus gets to him before he gets to himself."

Leo settles himself back in the seat. "You're an evangelist, you know."

I dismiss that thought right away. "Please. I need eyeliner and sequins and a Southern accent for that, don't I?"

"Not the way I see it. You need a heart. A certain kind of heart that sees things in people. You've got that."

Am I blushing? I feel as if I'm blushing. "Are you the same guy that slammed my office door Monday?"

"Same one. Just three days, twenty-six prayers and a triple cheeseburger later." Leo looks as though he wants to say more, as though he feels there's some kind of apology that needs to be said, but he is stopping himself. There's a moment of quiet between us.

"I don't know that you did anything bad, Leo. It's just that you caught me off guard

Monday. Way off guard. And I wasn't exactly cordial to you, either."

Leo leans forward to rest his elbows on the table. He has a tan pin-striped shirt on today, crisp and elegant against his black pants. "What do you say we start over?"

"Back to banana milk shake number one?" Back before cereal and *The Underdog Show* and iguana-sitting? I narrowly escaped the first time. Do I want to go back there?

Leo's eyes are one hundred percent high voltage charisma. "Somewhere between lizard-sitting and door-slamming."

Chapter Sixteen

Adding up...badly

Friday night, I open my door to see Kyle standing there, holding another huge bouquet of flowers. This time he is in a soft blue sweater, pushed up at the sleeves, and black jeans. Definitely a compelling tableau.

"Am I early?" he says, staring down at my feet, which I realize have no shoes on them.

"No, no, it's just me." I take the bouquet from him, noticing that both he and the flowers smell extremely nice. "Sit down. Let me get something for these and I'll just be a minute or so."

With Kyle safely stashed in my living

room, I dart around the apartment finding a vase, brushing my teeth, checking to make sure I have both earrings in and dabbing on a bit of perfume. He's staring at the Emmy on my bookshelf when I return.

"Is this real?" he asks, reaching out to touch it.

For a moment I find that an odd question, until I remember that there probably *are* people in Los Angeles with faux Emmys on their shelves—this isn't a city known for its authenticity.

"Yep, from the first season."

"Wow. I would think you'd have half a dozen of these by now."

"Thanks for the compliment, but they're rather hard to come by. That one's a special ensemble award we got before they knew what to do with prime-time animation. We didn't have any competition back then. Now we have loads of it."

Kyle turns to me and smiles. "You're amazing, you know that?"

I could get used to this. "Thanks. I'm ready now." I point to my feet, which now have shoes. Darling new shoes I purchased on my way home from work, which is the real reason I was late.

"Okay then, let's get going. I'm dying for you to meet everybody."

Kyle's family is the kind that should be on a cereal box. His sister has cute kids, a lovely home, a charming and successful husband—it's West Coast domestic perfection, right down to the adorable exotic-breed dog. Looking around me in the living room, hearing the upbeat chatter and taking in all the decorative splendor, I can understand why Kyle might get competitive. This is one older sister who has her act together. Who's got all the components of a successful life singing in perfect harmony.

That's one benefit of being an only child: no sibling rivalry. Of course, it also means there's no one to deflect attention. Your parents watch your every move, matching it against some internal checklist they've created for your personal, professional and spiritual happiness. No, not happiness. *Success.* Like every other person making a modest living in the entertainment industry, I've discovered the mile-wide gap between what makes me happy and what my parents view as success. Mom and Dad are probably still wondering when I'll settle down and get a real job. Not to mention that Mom's bought two puppies in an effort to squelch her desire for grandchildren.

Forcing such introspection from my mind, I survey the room—I know a few people in the crowd. There's Kyle's sister, niece and nephew. There's the technician who worked the control booth when we made the recordings. Everyone else is staring at me discreetly, whispering what looks like, "Honey, there's the girl Kyle brought." I'm feeling a bit on display, but it's not entirely unpleasant. Kyle's beaming. His hand hasn't left my side, elbow, arm or back the entire evening.

I like being doted upon.

About an hour into things, the first moment of pressure arrives. Actually, it's Kyle's parents who do the arriving. If he told me his mom and dad were going to be here, I didn't register it. Meeting the sister and more church friends is one thing. Meeting the parents is quite a different circumstance. The DEFCON of dating.

"Lindy, this is my Mom. Mom, this is Lindy." Kyle's hand is making small circles on my back. He's nervous. He wants her to like me.

"Delighted to meet you. Martha Tannon. Kyle's told me so much about you." She's a bit on the socially formal side, but her smile is genuine, as is her handshake.

Be charming. Be calm and charming. "Thanks. Your daughter has a lovely home."

"Danielle does have a way with decorating, doesn't she? I don't know where she finds the time with all she does."

"Oh," says Kyle, giving his mom a kiss on the cheek. It's so cute. "I have a feeling she learned it somewhere."

A boy who likes his mother? Do they even exist anymore?

"Beware, Miss Edwards, my son is quite the charmer." Martha laughs, and I swear in one more second she is going to reach up and ruffle Kyle's hair. "So, Kyle tells me you're on TV."

"*Arborville,* Mom. Lindy's the voice of Maggie Hoot on *Arborville.*"

"So I've heard. How fascinating."

And it would be. If this were not the twentieth time I've heard that this evening. Kyle has been touting my résumé a bit.

But he wants everyone to like me. He wants his mother to like me. How can you argue with that?

We're still chatting when Mr. Tannon, a tanned, fit man with a loud voice, saunters over with a beverage for his wife, "So, Kyle, is this your pretty little celebrity?"

We have now moved from "touting a bit" to "touting too much." Still, I'm okay with that. I think. I may need to have a talk with Kyle about high-visibility careers and relationships.

Things get dicey, though, when the touting doesn't seem to stop. Mr. Tannon is droning on in salesmanship tones about what is evidently viewed as Kyle's latest achievement; my brain begins to add things up.

And yes, folks, it is adding up. Badly.

The man hooted when I kissed him.

"Owl be seeing you" from the flower card. The convenient little slip up about the church announcements. "Just bring your voice and the pretty little package it comes in." Something between nausea and fury washes over me.

To Kyle, I'm not really Lindy.

I'm just the means to Maggie. To celebrity arm candy suitable for upstaging his big sister.

Is "trophy date" an actual term?

It was there all along, only I didn't see it. Kyle was so charming and so adorably repentant that I couldn't see it—or wouldn't see it. I finally get to a fifth date, with a guy who not only seems wonderfully normal but has a nice family, and what happens?

The thing I dread. The thing I hate most of all, the thing I try desperately to protect myself from.

A Maggie-izer.

How many times have I said that Maggie is what I do, not who I am? Now do you see why I just don't tell people? It gets in the way *every single time*. And do you know what's worst of all, what's saddest about this whole episode?

I don't even think Kyle knows he's doing it. It's not even a conscious decision—he can't help himself. He's still standing next to me, oblivious, practically ribbing his dad as they talk about what a catch I am. He probably thinks I'm flattered that he's told everyone.

How did I not see this coming? I'm so on guard for this. How did Kyle sneak under the radar? Why did I let such a stunning set of eyes and a couple of bouquets of flowers dupe me into thinking this time would be different?

I was wrong. So wrong. So fooled.

I risk one look at Kyle and his broad smile as he suggests, "Hey, you know, I taped the episode last night. We could get everyone to watch it. You could do a live commentary like on those movie DVDs."

And I know. I know for sure that if *Arborville* left the airwaves tomorrow, I'd fade from his view. I'd cease to be exciting.

Because I'm not Lindy Edwards, I'm an achievement. A notch on the scorecard of familial success. *Look at Kyle, he's dating a celebrity, sort of. Maybe he'll get his life together after all.*

I bought new shoes for this?

I can't get out of here fast enough. Before anyone says Maggie's trademark "And don't you come back here!" or one unfortunate soul utters the words "Do her!" I pry myself out of Kyle's manipulative grasp and ask for directions to the bathroom.

Once inside this shiny palace of pink marble with polished brass fixtures, stinking of potpourri, I yank my cell phone from my purse and hit the speed dial for Nigel's mobile.

"Darling!"

"Call me in ten minutes and start yelling about how I have to go back to the studio. I'll meet you there."

"Mr. Bouquet turning into a stack of thorns?"

"*Not now,* Nigel. Just save me. I'll buy you dinner—I'll buy you another iguana— if you just meet me looking panicked at the studio in half an hour."

"No worries, hon. I'm still here. Working on a script." The drama falls from his voice for a moment. "You okay?"

"No. Look, just call my cell in ten minutes, okay? No, make it five. Just get me *out of here.*"

"You want me to come get you?"

That'd be worse, that's for sure. Once this crowd gets a hold of the genius behind *Arborville,* it'll take weeks for us to make it out the front door. "No! Trust me, you don't want to see this. Just call. *Promise me* you'll call, Nigel."

"Four minutes, fifty-nine seconds, and counting."

"You're a doll."

"So they keep telling me."

Five minutes. I can stand this for five minutes. *Lord, save me from myself. Save me from the way I feel. How did this happen? Just get me through the next five minutes, that's all I ask. The bigger prayers will come later, just get me out this door quick, in one piece and without a big scene.*

Prayers completed, I decide to go find the most delicious-looking piece of food on that buffet table and spend four minutes eating it, making sure Kyle is within earshot when my phone rings.

Four minutes and twenty-seven seconds later, Kyle finds me halfway through my second brownie. He is surrounded by Marcy and a gaggle of preteen children. Good to have him nearby—within clear earshot—but then he says, "Hey Lindy, I know you don't like to do Maggie, but Marcy and I were just—"

Ring!

Before anyone can realize I have secretly left it on speakerphone, I shrug my shoulders and hit the talk button on my cell phone, now conveniently clipped to the waistband of my pants. "Hello?"

"Lindy, if you don't get your high-priced tailfeathers up here to the studio in two minutes…" I'll leave the rest of Nigel's colorful description and vocabulary to your imagination.

Oops. Tactical error.

If I wanted to guarantee a swift exit, I called the right guy. Nigel's broadcast tirade is definitely R-rated, and half the living room has now heard his stunning vocabulary.

Including the smiling young faces now shell-shocked and staring at Uncle Kyle.

Chapter Seventeen

Not falling for it

It will not surprise you, I'm guessing, to learn Sophia found me waiting outside Fiber Content when it opened Saturday morning. I needed some new yarn. I didn't want the browns and greens warring with each other anymore on my needles. I don't want to have anything to do with that sweater anymore. The brown kept showing up more than the green, and I used that. It's what I wanted, I realized—the brown to dominate. I wanted the sweater to decide for me between Kyle and Leo.

Actually, when I think about it, I *let* the

sweater decide for me. Yes, well, God and I have had a good long conversation about that particular recurring problem of mine. I have the Lord of the Universe looking out for the good of my soul, and I ask a hunk of sheep hair to make decisions for me? Again?

Is it any wonder I ended up in this mess?

I wanted to return it, but Sophia wouldn't let me. Not that it's against store policy— she's bent store policy for me dozens of times—but she insists I'll want it some day.

"Tuck it way back in your closet," she said, stroking my hand as I told her the whole story. "You'll come back to it. It called you once, it'll call to you again."

I doubt it. Still, it felt good to sit there, sipping coffee, surrounded by color and texture, and get the whole story out. Even if she does get a little *woo-woo* about her yarn, Sophia's still the cheapest therapy I know.

She had a lot of red yarn out for Valentine's Day, but I steered way clear of that. I chose a purple yarn and a shawl pattern. No fancy loops, no tricky stitches to confound me, just the soothing rhythm of endless simple stitches.

I tossed Kyle's flowers when I came home. A waste of botany, I know, but it felt good. I feel so stupid, so duped, that any authoritative action feels comforting. I sorted my closet, too. I now have the most organized dateless pseudocelebrity wardrobe in town.

This was also a week for cleaning. For purging. For ridding my life of the choking deadwood keeping me down. Angry cleaning is always the most effective. No year-old magazine, no old Christmas card, no unread catalog was safe from me this week. By Tuesday, I had nothing in my apartment left to clean, so I grabbed both big garbage cans from the studio kitchen and went to town on my office.

The result was a pile of garbage in the middle of my office floor that represented half a forest of useless paper. If I could have, I'd have taken a match to it and lit a ceremonial bonfire.

Everyone caught on that I was not in a chatty mood this week, and left me alone.

Almost everyone.

Just before lunch, with the papers still strewn about my office, Leo appears in my doorway. "Working through a few issues?" he says, offering me a coffee cup.

"Excuse me?" I take the coffee because it'd be rude not to.

"Angry cleaner. Takes one to know one. I wash my car when I'm angry. Tick me off, and my car is clean enough to host a surgical procedure."

"Thanks for sharing." I'm not in the mood to deal with any member of the male species this week. "Look, I'm kind of busy. Is there something you need?"

Leo looks around the room, a funny expression on his face. I choose to ignore it. "Okay then. See you later."

On Thursday, when I walked back into my office after taping, there was a banana shake and a box of Cap'n Crunch waiting for me on my desk. No note, no Leo, just the shake and cereal.

I'm not falling for this. Do you hear me? It's not going to work. Leo is still a member of the male species, and he's still from the Evil Empire. No matter his charm, I can't let myself forget why Leo is here in the first place.

Nigel told me this morning he's got a script coming up that will put us back on the top. He's done it before, so I believe him. No one's going to take that away from us just because some advertisers think we're "edgy."

Edgy is good. Edgy makes people think. Edgy brings about change. John the Baptist was edgy. Paul was edgy. I'd even go so far as to say Jesus was edgy. No one ever makes great social strides by staying comfortable.

Okay, Miss Lindy will now step down off her soapbox.

You're probably wondering what happened to Kyle. Well, Kyle's probably wondering what happened to Kyle, too. We had a phone conversation Sunday afternoon, but I'm not sure I explained things well. It's hard to accuse someone of liking you for your celebrity status when you're not really much of a celebrity and he doesn't even realize that's what he's been doing. If I hadn't had repeated experience with this sort of thing, I doubt I'd have recognized it for months.

Friday morning, my computer registers an urgent e-mail when I turn it on.

From lcorbin@netrate.com.

One sentence. Are you okay?

What am I supposed to do with that? And when did I give Leo my e-mail address? I decide on brevity: Rough week. Bad date. All better now, I'm fine. Thanks for asking.

I go back to proofreading a bio for the new Web site until my computer dings again. Nobody cleans that viciously when they're fine. Want to have lunch?

I glare at my computer for a moment, crafting a suitable reply. It wasn't vicious, it was comprehensive. Can't do lunch, I'm busy.

It's only a minute before another ding. You're avoiding me.

This is exactly what I don't need. No, I'm not. I'm just busy. Thanks for the cereal by the way, maybe I'll have a bowl for lunch.

At 1:15 I get another e-mail from Leo. How was lunch with the Captain? Crunchy?

This guy doesn't know when to let up. Don't you have careers to destroy somewhere? Slow week up at the Evil Empire? I resist the urge to utter "Take that!" as I hit the reply button.

I do not receive another e-mail in reply.

That is, until 3:30, when he e-mails again—this time in the shorthand of someone typing with their thumbs on their PDA rather than a keyboard. In a mtg. 8 this wk. Boring. Coffee @ 4?

Thanks to modern technology, adults everywhere have returned to the grade-school behavior of passing notes in class. I've seen Jason do it in the middle of table reads. I'm trying to stay annoyed, really I am.

I can't, I reply. I could actually, and I'd almost like to, but I've decided it's best not to have anything to do with men for a while.

Can't or won't?

Are you always this bullheaded?

Goal-oriented. Coffee?

No, Leo. Bad idea.

I hear no dings for the rest of the afternoon. Even though I have a tinge of regret, I'm mostly glad to have put that matter to rest.

I'm packing up my stuff to leave for the weekend when the computer dings. Four times.

There are four consecutive, identical e-mails from Leo.

Look out your window.

Look out your window.

Look out your window.

Look out your window.

Annoyed but curious, I slide open the blinds of my window to see Leo's car sitting in the parking lot, with Leo in it, flashing his lights.

I hit Reply: You're a strange and deluded man, Leo Corbin.

There is a bit of a pause before Leo types: I need to see you again.

Leo… I type, unable to come up with anything else. I really don't want to get into this, especially via e-mail.

Another long pause, and I can see Leo madly banging into the open laptop on his passenger seat. I can't stop thinking about you. I know it's complicated, but I don't care.

Complicated? Things could get really ugly, I reply, checking twice to see if anyone's standing in my doorway.

I know, but… I don't want to walk away from this just yet.

I can't stop myself from asking. Especially after this last week. What if you cancel the show?

I don't know, Leo types in reply.

We HAVE to think about that, I type back, banging my keys hard.

Leo's reply is not what I expect: Please, can I take you to dinner tomorrow night?

I stare at the blinking cursor, arguing with myself. One part of me saying "Leo is different!" while another part of me argues "You always think 'this guy will be different.' And where has it gotten you?" I risk a glance out the window to see, all too clearly, Leo staring at my window. Even from this distance, I can see the cool green of his eyes. Then he types again.

A normal date. No Nigels, no iguanas, no network.

Then, with his persuasion practically soaking the airwaves, comes the words, Please. One.

It's a bad idea. I'm biting my lip as I type, fighting the urge to give in to this tidal wave of blatant inducement.

No kidding. Say yes anyway.

I can't help but smile. Even though every ounce of me knows better, I type, Are you always this obsessed?

One word returns: No.

"Don't do it. Don't give in." Voices in my head are screaming cautionary tales. Then one small thought breaks through:

Don't let Kyle make you like this. I hold my breath and type: OK.

Leo must have hit the panic button on his key chain, because suddenly his car lights flash and his horn beeps repeatedly. I giggle, unsure if he did this on purpose.

Oops! comes across my screen, and I laugh. 7 p.m. follows.

Where? I type back.

I'll let you know.

Leo's car engine roars to life. He's leaving? Now? Wait, Leo… I type and say to the window at the same time. This is way too much unknown for me. I don't even like grab bags.

You'll love this. Trust me.

Doesn't he know the two words you should never say to a control freak are *"Trust me"*?

Chapter Eighteen

Moon over Los Angeles

It's past five—less than two hours away from the date in question, and I have not one clue as to what's about to happen. Not one, do you hear me? I don't know if I'm doing sushi or opera or sunset on the beach. The suspense is about to do me in when my phone rings.

It's Suzann. "Sooo?" she sings into the phone.

Tactical error number one was telling Suzann. Although really, I don't see how you can fault me for that. I get to play the real-life version of Mystery Date; I've got to dish the details with someone. This could be a very romantic evening. I'm actually being pursued. Wooed. Courted. Romanced....

Ahem. Back to Suzann. Bad idea. I'm watching the clock as it is, and having Suzann call me every hour—even while she's on the air!—and say, "Sooo?" as in "has he clued you in yet?" is not helpful.

"Nothing."

"Nothing? It's after five!"

Thanks Suz, I really wasn't watching the clock without your cue. "I'm aware of this."

"Maybe you should be at a spa. Doing your nails or applying a pore-reducing mask or something."

I have brown hair. I have olive-toned skin. Which means I have large pores. Tiny-pored people with fabulous blond hair—people like Suzann—never seem to understand that two hundred bottles of expensive mud simply will not undo two thousand years of Mediterranean genetics. I like a good facial as much as the next woman, but I understand the limits of modern science. Besides, I've already done my nails. And my toes. And my makeup.

Twice. I'm in my perfectly adaptable black jersey ready-for-anything dress. This is as ready as it gets.

"Leo said he would come here. I told you that at ten o'clock when you called. And at two o'clock, and at three.

"He's not giving you much—"

"Suz." I'm entitled to cut her off, I think. "If you can't think of something calm-inducing to say, just stop…" I fall silent because there's a knock on my door. I look through the peephole to see a messenger guy with a big gift-wrapped box. "I'll call you back."

"What! No, you can't…" I hear Suz's voice rant on as I put down the receiver.

Whatever it is, it's heavy. The guy slides it onto my hall table and holds out papers for signatures. I run through the options as I sign my name. Too big and too heavy for jewelry or clothes. Food? Sculpture? My mind is drawing a complete blank on objects dense and romantic.

I stand there after tipping the messenger, staring, pondering the possibilities. I don't want to rush this. It could be a pivotal moment in my life. I prepare myself to be romanced. The scene playing through my brain right now is the scene where Richard Gere gives the red gown and jewels to Julia Roberts in *Pretty Woman*. Pure, unadulterated romantic fantasy. There is a huge, aching part of me that wants to see what happens when Leo Corbin pulls out all the stops.

That's real ribbon on that package. Not gift-wrap ribbon, but actual cloth ribbon. Like the kind they give you at Tiffany's. Or Godiva.

I pull back the red-and-yellow paisley wrapping paper to reveal a perfectly plain white box. No clues there.

I slide one finger under the lid and lift. Red tissue paper in crisp folds. I'm still stumped.

Delicately, carefully, I untuck the tissue to reveal my courtship.

It's cloth.

Basic, bright colored cloth. If I didn't know any better, I'd say it was a...

Oh.

Oh, goodness. It is. In the name of all that's splendid and female, it can't be.

It's a bowling shirt.

196 My So-Called Love Life

You heard me, a bowling shirt.

Great. It's not *Pretty Woman,* it's *The Honeymooners.* You know, the episode where he buys her a bowling ball for her birthday because it's what he really wants and…

Oh, no. Heavy box. *No, please, no.*

There's a bright red bowling ball in the box under my shirt.

Can I cry now?

I don't care that the shirt has Leo's Lizards on the back, and that it's monogrammed with my name on the front.

I don't care that the ball is brand-new and even has my initials on it.

I'd sooner die than put any of this on and go to the address listed on that stupid instruction card poking out of one finger hole of that stupid bowling ball.

Leo Corbin is a stupid, annoying, arrogant knuckle-dragger of a man if he thinks this is what I'd call romance.

And the only reason I'm hauling all this stuff over to that address is so that I can tell him just that. Did his sisters teach him nothing? I'm thinking, no matter how unscriptural, that the most appropriate place for this bowling ball right now would be dropped squarely on Leo Corbin's foot.

At considerable velocity. With malice aforethought.

I'm grunting every despicable name I can imagine as I stuff that ostentatious shirt back into the box over that obnoxious hunk of vinyl, and yank open my apartment door.

Leo is lucky he chose someplace clear across town at rush hour. The drive gives me time to calm down—slightly. I entertain visions of Leo explaining to the emergency room nurse how his fabulous date ended in contusion rather than courtship. She'll just frown and shake her head—no woman on this planet would find this highly romantic. No, sir, this is a gag gift, not a…what did he call it? A "normal date"? If this is what he calls a normal date…

Ten Pin Alley, with its cheesy Western theme, is about as romantic as a landfill. According to my dastardly little instruction sheet, I'm supposed to check in with Dino— yes, folks, that seems to be his real name, according to the chipped plastic name tag he bears—to announce my arrival.

"Where is he?" I demand, slamming my box onto the counter. If he hands me one of the pairs of shoes he's currently dousing with spray disinfectant, it's going to get ugly.

Dino stops midspray, eyes me and pops his chewing gum. "You Lindy?"

"You get many ball-toting women coming in here?"

Dino stares at me blankly. Obviously, my brain is not operating. Of course he gets ball-toting women in here. It's a bowling alley.

He must think I'm completely bonkers. I am, too, for having thought for even one moment of going along with this thing.

"He ain't here."

Figures. "Oh, just fine. That's really—"

"He said you should wait for him, that he'd be right back."

Maybe knock off a couple of frames while I'm waiting?

As if hearing my thoughts, Dino leans over the counter to stare at my feet. "You want shoes?"

"No, I do not want shoes. I don't want any of this, I just want to tell Leo—"

Dino is laughing now, evidently finding my anger amusing. "You can't. He ain't here."

"You said that already."

"Hey, maybe you want to leave him a note if you ain't staying? He said I should keep you here but if you're so ticked off…"

Now there's a quandary: stay here to personally tell Leo off, or write a note and not have to see his conniving face again? Let's see, which would be more effective? Which would be more satisfying?

Dino shifts his gaze to behind me. "Good evening, Mr. Corbin." His pleasant tone clashes with his Brooklynese accent.

"Evening, Dino."

I whip around, ready to lash into Leo.

And stop dead at the sight.

Chapter Nineteen

What's behind door number two

Leo is standing in the bowling alley doorway.

In a gorgeous dark suit and a dazzling sky-blue tie.

He could not look more handsome if he were in a tuxedo. Still, I want to strangle him. So I stand here, stuck somewhere between awed and angry, completely at a loss for what to do next.

"Okay," says Leo, taking a step back and rubbing his hand across his chin. "*Not* the reaction I was shooting for." In the unsettled tone of his voice, I sense that Leo *has* pulled out all the stops, expecting to "bowl me over"—pun intended, and he's flustered that it didn't work.

Dino decides to break the ice. "You spent a lot of money to tick off a lady, Leo."

Leo seems to be a regular at Ten Pin Alley. Is that good news or bad news?

Leo looks at me unsteadily. "Do you want to know what's behind door number two or should I just back away slowly?"

"You want I should tell her how much we charge for rush orders, Leo? It's double, lady. I got a lotta customers would kill for a ball like that. You otta…"

Leo raises a hand, still locked on my eyes. "*Not helping,* Dino…."

"Yeah, sure. I…um…should go clean something, I think."

Receiving no response from either Leo or myself, Dino slinks off, muttering what I am sure was "crazy kids," to go find something to clean. Trust me, he won't have to look far.

"I'd feel a lot better if you said something." Leo's fingers are tapping on the box he's holding.

"A large percentage of women," I begin slowly, "would not rank bowling among the most romantic of activities."

Leo glances from side to side, nodding a bit. "Botched it. Check."

"I have a feeling where you were heading with this, but it didn't work. Not under these conditions. Not in the slightest."

He stills. "Yep, I see that."

"Now, the suit—the very nice, very dashing suit by the way—does work highly in your favor."

Leo risks a step in my direction. "Boy, am I glad to hear that."

"So, on the possibility that this evening can *only* improve, I'm going to at least look at what's behind door number two before I stomp off into the sunset."

"Good. I'll take that. That's good." He looks so relieved it's almost comical. "And, you know, if you want to take what's behind door number two *and* stomp off into the sunset, I'd deserve that, too."

Big, awkward pause.

"So," I cue him, "this would be the part where you give me the box and apologize."

"Oh. Right. The box. This is for you. I'm sorry you feel tricked. I wanted us to have some fun… but…it's *crystal clear* we're not having any fun here. So…I think…I hope you'll like this better." Befuddled. He's *befuddled*. How dare it look so attractive on the guy.

It dawns on me, as Leo hands me the box, that some part of me is rooting for him. Despite all my reservations, some deep corner of my heart wants him to get this right, to salvage this evening.

Holding my breath, I open the box.

It's a shawl. A lush, hand-knit shawl in a deep emerald green. It's absolutely beautiful.

"I saw you knitting in the studio one day," he offers.

It's a masterful piece of knitting. Far beyond my skill, but something I'd have picked out myself. I hold it up, and it drapes around my hands in thick, soft swirls. "Much better." I glance up at Leo, unable to hide my pleasure.

"You can't believe how glad I am to hear that." The million-watt smile is back. "We've got eight o'clock dinner reservations, if you're willing to let me start over...*over* over, that is. Your call. If you say so, I'll just leave. But..." he stops, stuffing his hands in his pockets instead of finishing the sentence.

He means it. Really. I can't ignore that.

I can't bring myself to just chuck it all and walk away. Too much of me wants to believe him. But can I trust him? And if not now, when? If I walk away now I'll never know if I *could* have trusted him.

But I don't want to trust him. Do I? Leo does things to me that I both love and loathe. I'm never in control when he's around. And yet it feels amazing. And not. All wrong and irresistible at the same time.

Still, there are a boatload of obstacles here, and one great evening won't wipe them away.

Even one *really* great evening. I take the shawl and wrap it over my shoulders. I'd be lying if I said I didn't adore it.

"It looks wonderful on you," Leo says quietly. "Please keep it."

"Let's go to dinner," I say before I can talk myself out of it.

Leo grins, and nods.

"I'll watch your cars so nothin' happens to them whiles you're gone. And I'll just hang on to these." Dino takes the box with my shirt and bowling ball and slides them under the counter.

"Sure." Leo is still grinning.

"Cars?" I say, wondering about the plural.

"Limo." Still grinning.

"You hired a limousine for this evening?"

"Outside."

Sure enough, behind Leo I can see the sleek black silhouette of a limousine. Yes, stops are definitely being pulled out here. I'm warming up to it. I can see where Leo gets his professional reputation for pulling things back from the brink of disaster.

On the seat inside the limo is a single calla lily. I pick it up and admire its retro sleekness. It's a Bette Davis kind of flower, with a vintage elegance. A perfect touch. Leo comes around to the other side of the car and settles himself in beside me. There's room for six other people in here, but I don't really notice it. I notice him, and the way he's looking at me. "You're star-ing," I manage to say without giggling.

"I know." More staring. Gaping, even.

"I like the wrap."

"Me, too."

I feel like I'm under a very bright spot-light. Intoxicating, but a bit uncomfortable. "Where are we going for dinner?"

"Campanile."

Campanile. One of the most romantic, most expensive restaurants in town. People go there to propose. Movie stars go there. Scoring a table on a Saturday night at Campanile is a social Mt. Everest. Leo must have pulled serious strings to make this happen on twenty-four-hours' notice. "Well, it seems you *do* know what consti-tutes a romantic date. You just take your time getting there."

Leo smiles. "Speaking of taking time to get there, it won't be a quick drive on a Saturday night, so I've arranged for an ap-petizer of sorts." Leaning forward, he opens the small refrigerator—the *refriger-ator!*—by the front seat to reveal two foam cups with straws.

Bearing the Hogan's Diner logo.

"Banana shake?" He hands me a cup. "I thought about champagne glasses, but decided this presents less of a risk to both shawl and suit."

Such an attention to detail fills our evening from the choice of table to the food to the way Leo holds the door open for me. My resistance is softening under the power of this man's courtship. I feel as if I'm in a movie, or that the alarm will go off any minute and I'll wake up to an ordinary Saturday.

"Do you miss Boston?" Leo asks when I choose Boston cream pie from the restaurant's exquisite dessert cart.

"Sometimes. There are days when I wish my parents were closer. When I want a frappe or fried clams or just some slice of my childhood." I take a bite of the pie. A well done Boston cream pie is one of the most perfect joys on earth. "Then there are the days where I'm thankful there's two time zones between me and my mother, and that I don't have to keep an ice scraper in my glove compartment."

Leo chuckles into his apple tart. "I remember snow. Actually, I remember shoveling snow. And breaking a leg skiing in college. Not a real fan of snow. You?"

"I like snow the way we have it. If I get a craving for it, I can drive up into the mountains and get my fix. That's snow on my terms. Snow on demand."

"How'd you lose the accent?"

"The Bostonese? It's not gone, it's just on-demand, too." I adopt the broad tones of my homeland for show. "I can *pahk my cahr in Hahvahd yahd* any old time I feel like it. I can do seven other U.S. accents, too. Plus, six foreigns and one completely made up accent that doesn't sound like anywhere. I could prank call my own parents and they'd never know it was me."

Leo thinks for a minute before asking, "You get on okay with your parents? Are they proud of you and all?"

There is a tone in his voice, a distance in his eyes, that tells me instantly that Leo's answer to his own question would be "no."

"They love me. They want me happy. They just can't really understand how making silly voices all day does that. I was supposed to go to college, get a job in radio or television journalism, stay in New England, marry the junior vice president and pop out a few grandchildren. They don't know what to make of *this* life."

"But they love you. I mean, they let you know they love you." I'm not even sure if Leo knows he's said that out loud, there's such yearning in his voice.

"I'm an only child," I say, injecting a laugh into my answer because I don't want the tinge of sadness to stay in the air. "They have to. They have to dote on me and obsess over my life and call too often. It's in the rule book. You don't think I ended up an entertaining control freak with well-balanced parenting, did you? Trust me," I say, adopting Dino's New York bark, "I got issues."

Leo raises an eyebrow, and I see the smile sneak back across his face. "Banana shake, Boston cream pie, cheese curls..."

So Nigel told him about the cheese curls. How does Leo bring things out of people so easily? "Speaking of issues, Mr. Corbin, what's with the ten-pin obsession? The shirts are one thing, but I can't really see you as a bowling kind of guy," I finally inquire, in desperate need of dialogue to squelch the growing giddiness.

"I picked it up in college."

"But bowling? You seem more the racquetball kind of guy."

"I work all day with the racquetball kind of guys. By the end of the week you need a shot of real life. Nobody at Ten Pin has ever seen me in a suit, and I like that."

For the first time, I catch the faintest hint of twang in Leo's voice. There's something else lurking under all that high-octane polish. "Where did you grow up?"

Leo hesitates before answering. "Tennessee. Outside of Memphis."

"I thought I heard a little bit of that in your voice. Leo Corbin, there's a little bit of cowboy somewhere inside that power suit."

"Hey, I worked all through college to lose that accent, you know. Without professional training."

"I do voices for a living. I'm a professional. And even then, it took me weeks to pick up on it."

Leo actually looks uncomfortable. Why? "It's no big deal. Tennessee's a perfectly fine state. They gave us Elvis Presley, Gibson guitars and deep-fried everything, among many other fine domestic products." When he still grimaces, I add, "Why keep it such a secret?"

"I don't."

"You do. You didn't want to tell me just now."

"That's not…"

"And you said back in the park how much you were ready to get out of Hicksville."

I can see Leo deciding whether or not to keep denying. Finally, running his finger around the rim of his water glass, he admits, "People in L.A. don't take you seriously with cowboy boots on."

"Come off it. You're smarter than that. Trust me, Leo, people take you *very* seriously. I don't think accents or footwear would make a bit of difference in that."

"Which is why you don't work at the network. That stuff matters, whether it makes the world a nice place or not. Come on, Lindy, think about the people you work with. It's not exactly a corporate environment. Being odd is a professional asset in your business. In my world, you've got to look powerful to get power."

"Is that what you're after, Leo? Power?" There are moments, when Leo talks like that, where the hardened executive comes roaring out of his features. There's a steel edge in his voice. I am reminded that this is a man who takes control. A man who gets what he wants.

Leo leans in and looks at me intently. "Yes. And no. Not power by itself, but power as a means to an end. How many times have you gone to a movie, or watched a TV show, and been heartsick by what passes for entertainment these days? Don't you remember going to the movies and feeling like if the hero could conquer the world, you could, too?" Leo stops fiddling with the glass and grabs my hand. "I want that back. I want to be the guy who brings that back. I'm sick of watching really good shows, with really good reviews, die anyway to bad ratings because they won't pander. I *do* want power because I want the power to keep the good stuff on the air. I want the power to green-light a project *because* it's got no sex or violence, not in spite of it."

How often do you get to hear someone speak the cry of their heart? Even before they've realized it's erupted out of them? I have no doubt this is what Leo was born to do. There is a fire in Leo's eyes that makes me believe he'll succeed. I'm pulled in by the conviction in his voice and the power he knows he wields, the power he's fought to wield.

Whether I want to or not, I begin falling. For Leo. Not just because he's handsome or funny or powerful, but because of what I just saw. His heart. Because of what he fights for, what he believes in and the uphill battle he's taken on. It's a nearly im-possible quest.

But you know me, I've got a thing for *Underdog*.

"I believe you." I tighten my hand around his. My heart feels like it's uncurl-ing, slipping out of my grip.

"Good." He smiles, after a momentary

pause that conveys how much he seemed to need to hear that. "That's one," he says softly. "A few hundred media moguls more, and we're golden." His eyes pull me in, and I offer no resistance.

"How come," Leo continues as his other hand finds its way across the table to mine, "there's always something between us?"

"Hmm?"

"Every time I want to kiss you, there's something between us." His fingers are making slow circles on the back of my palm. "Last time it was an angry iguana. Now it's an entire restaurant table. How come?"

How do you answer that? Having a handsome man declare his intent to kiss you is almost as good as the best kiss itself. Having him declare it with *that* look on his face pretty much makes any resistance useless.

The impulse comes over me in a heartbeat. "Hey," I whisper, "Do you think Ten Pin is still open?"

Leo looks as if he's been waiting all night to hear that. "It's closed already. But Dino's there, waiting for us, just in case

Allie Pleiter 215

we'd like a private lane to cap the evening off." He grins and motions for the waiter.

"You know," I say as Leo pulls me by the hand to the open limousine door, "I'm really awful at bowling."

Suddenly, I'm in a long, slow, send-the-world-spinning kiss. "I couldn't care less," he whispers.

I believe him.

"Ha! Beat that!"

I have, by some extraordinary set of circumstances, achieved a 7-10 split. Twice.

Leo, shirt rolled up at the sleeves, tie hanging undone around his collar, produces a disbelieving smirk. "I distinctly heard you say you were 'really awful' at this. I am not seeing really awful here."

I extend my hands and twirl, runway style, in front of him. "I am wearing a dress, a bowling shirt and shoes the color of Astro Turf. Leo, I am the visual personification of 'really awful.'"

He has this laugh, this deep bell chime of a laugh, that vibrates right through my spine. "And you are just *now* concluding that fashion and bowling do not go hand in hand?"

"Hey," calls Dino, who is engaged in pin-to-pin combat with the limo driver a discreet six lanes away, "I heard that. Aw, for cryin' out loud, look what you made me do." Dino knocks down a pathetic single pin, producing a victory whoop from the limo driver.

"Well," I counter, pointing to Leo, "your shoes don't look so…so…enthusiastic." Leo's shoes actually look like shoes, whereas mine resemble neon Vegas signs.

"The serious bowler owns his own serious equipment." As if to reinforce the fact, Leo picks up his ball and hoists it from hand to hand. I should point out here that Leo's ball is a deep, intoxicating blue. A midnight, starry-night blue that looks rather stunning against the white and black of his attire. I would not have thought a guy could look this good bowling. Then again, before tonight, I would not have thought a lot of things about Leo Corbin.

I tug my red-black-and-yellow shirt and point to my lipstick-red ball. Leo may have a Cary Grant look about him, but I'm feeling more like Lucille Ball. "You call this serious?"

Leo does not answer. Instead, after a look that makes me gulp, he pauses for one brief moment before lunging into the fluid motion that sends his ball barreling down the lane to obliterate every pin in its path.

Chapter Twenty

The biggest risk ever

Ah, Sunday. I've had a good postchurch nap and I'm knitting away the afternoon. Back at my first sweater, simply enjoying the interplay of colors rather than investing myself in it. I've just finished a perfect row when the phone rings.

"Hi, you." Leo's voice is low and musical. The sensation of it washes over me.

I drop the knitting and swing my legs around to curl up on the couch. "Hey there."

"I was useless at church this morning."

"Really," I reply, inappropriately pleased to hear it. "How come?"

"I kept yawning for starters, and then my mind kept wandering toward a certain someone."

I stifle a yawn of my own. "I'm gathering it wasn't the Apostle Paul filling your daydreams?"

Leo laughs softly, and the sound sparkles in my ear. "No, it wasn't."

I scoot down on the couch until I'm lying flat on my back. "I had a wonderful time last night, Leo. Really."

"Me, too. Although I'm still not sure I believe you're bad at bowling. You were far too good for my definition of 'really awful.'"

"Well, now that I have all this spiffy equipment, I suppose I'll have to take it up or something." I stare at the shirt and ball sitting in the middle of the floor where I dumped them last night. I fight the urge to go put the shirt on.

There's a small, surprisingly comfortable silence between us. "I had a really good time last night, Lindy."

I giggle. "I think we covered that already."

"Well—" he yawns "—maybe it bears repeating."

"Fine by me." I roll over to push myself up on my elbows. "Are you going to be at the table read tomorrow? I don't know how I'm going to pull this off. I'm not sure I can be cool and professional around you anymore."

"Well, you're off the hook for tomorrow at least. I was calling you to let you know I'll be up at the network through Wednesday. I won't be around to distract you or make you lose focus until Thursday's taping."

"Too late. I'm already distracted."

"I know the feeling. Hey, Lindy, what color is it that iguanas get when they meet someone they like?"

"Green." I'm smiling like an idiot. "Really bright green."

"Lindy?"

"Yes?"

"I'm really, *really* green."

"And fade to the credits." The producer's voice is tense as he reads the final direction on today's script.

The room is absolutely silent.

Except for Nigel, who's fidgeting over there in the corner, twirling a pen at high velocity. Waiting, obviously, for us all to expound on his artistic genius.

Like I said, the room is silent to the point of painful. None of us know what to say. Jason, who'd probably be cruel enough to say what we're all thinking, has already left the room. He tossed his script on the table ten minutes ago, lit up a cigarette in the conference room—a company no-no—and is probably already on the phone. Jason's agent is about to get a raging earful.

Why? Because Jason's dead.

Nigel killed off Dylan Weasel in this week's episode.

Actually, it's worse than that. Nigel wrote an episode where Dylan kills himself. Railroad tracks. Blood, gore, angst. There's a stage direction for the animated blood to appear as if it's splashing up on the television screen. When Nigel told me weeks ago he was going to have a death on the show, I thought he was taking us into newer, deeper subjects.

He did, sort of. The mourning and compassion between *Arborville*'s characters as they grieve is astounding. Heart-wrenching. But even that can't change how gory this episode feels. Plus, Nigel has just killed off the most popular character on the show. You can't get away with filing that under "artistic risk."

Osgood, who, as our executive producer is supposed to keep things like this from happening, looks as if he might be ill at any moment. Someone told me he's been here since 3:00 a.m. when the script showed up on everyone's doorstep. One of the other writers—the ones who evidently tried to talk Nigel out of this artistic time bomb—called Osgood when they failed to get Nigel to see reason.

"Well," Nigel says finally when no one seems to stop staring at him, "this ought to get their attention." He's looking right at Osgood.

"What do you think you're doing, Nigel?" Osgood says slowly.

"Taking the biggest risk television's ever seen." Nigel replies, settling back in his chair.

"You had Dylan kill himself," gasps

Kelly, who can usually be counted on to state the obvious. She has curled up her script and is currently wringing it with tense, manicured hands. "We *watch* Dylan kill himself. Nigel, it's disgusting."

"It's *shocking,*" Nigel corrects her.

Osgood puts his head in his hands. "We'll lose sponsors in droves."

Nigel tells Osgood—in quite graphic terms—what the sponsors can go do with themselves. People groan and shift uneasily in their seats—that is, those who haven't already gotten up and left. This is out of line, even for Nigel. Sure, I don't like the idea of Nigel killing off a character, but he's the kind of writer who could make even something like that poignant and sadly funny. And parts of this script are. But most of it is pure, ugly shock. Nigel's supposed to take us to the edge and pull back just in the nick of time. He's supposed to take risk, push our concept of what's acceptable, but then make the show brilliantly redeem itself. That's what Nigel does.

But he hasn't done it this time. Jason's dialogue was all sharp and nasty without a hint of even dark humor. Now that I think about it, I can't remember laughing once during the whole table read. That's never happened before. Fighting a rising sense of panic, I stand up and gather my papers.

"Lindy, baby, tell us what you thought," Nigel calls. He's still got his sunglasses on, so I can't see what's going on in his eyes. I'm not sure I even want to.

I have no witty reply. "You don't want to know," I say quietly, and get out of there as fast as I can.

I practically run to my office, and throw myself into a chair. *Take deep breaths. There's no reason to panic. It's one script. One bad script.* One really bad script in a slew of brilliant shows. Nigel's saved us before.

But that's just it: it's always Nigel's talent that pulls us back from the brink of disaster. We've come to expect that of him. We've come to trust him to do it over and over. Now that it's Nigel who's got his hand on the proverbial knife, who will save us now?

Suddenly, I remember the last thing I

said to Leo when he stormed out of my office that day. "Save us, Leo."

Leo's up at the network. Which means they must be doing some big-time decision making this week. *Oh, Nigel, couldn't you have picked a less disastrous time to lose your grip?*

I look up to see Kelly standing in my doorway. "Lindy, it's awful," she says. She looks on the verge of tears.

"It'll be okay," I say, not necessarily because I believe it, but because she looks as if she desperately needs to hear it. "Osgood will do something. Nigel will fix it. We'll be okay."

Kelly looks unconvinced. I motion for her to sit down. "Remember the molting episode?" Nigel's take on cosmetic surgery. I'm sure you can imagine what he did with that delicate issue—we were terrified for weeks until the great reviews came out about how insightful and honest the show was. "We were nervous then. It's just like that."

But it's not. I know it. Kelly senses it. Somewhere there's a psalm that covers this type of panic, but I can't remember a single verse of anything at the moment. "Want to go get some coffee?" I offer, just because I can't think of anything else to say.

"Sure," Kelly whimpers.

When we pass the tight knot of *Arborville* employees rattling around each other in the coffee room, I grab Kelly's arm. "How about we really go get some coffee. Let's get out of here." I'd just as soon be somewhere where Nigel can't ask my opinion right now.

"I can't think of a better idea, Lindy."

I knit in a crisis. I pray in a crisis. I eat in a crisis. Kelly shops in a crisis. While she dives into the shoe store next to our favorite local coffee bar, I walked around the block to have a long silent talk with God about the state of *Arborville*.

I can't believe this is what You wanted, Lord. I know I'm at Arborville *for a reason. What possible good could come from me watching it crumble around me? You must have a purpose for a script like this. Don't you? You gave me such a heart for this show, for these people. Suddenly everything's a mess. What would you have me do, Lord?*

My question went unanswered. I decided that the best thing I could do would be to just go home, get quiet and keep listening for that still, small voice. I head out without returning any messages or even looking at my mail.

Chapter Twenty-One

You know what they say...part II

"Come on, love, give us a ring up, will you? You left the studio before I could talk with you."

It's one of four messages Nigel's left on my answering machine this afternoon. I'm not answering my phone. I'm hiding out, praying when I can concentrate, and knitting when I can't. I've gotten so much knitting done I'll have this sweater finished by Thursday.

At around dinnertime, the call I've been dreading comes in. "Lindy? It's Leo. I just saw the script. Come on, Lindy, pick up.

I'm almost sure you're home— I know you're not at the studio." He waits for me to pick up, and I almost do. I'm just reaching for the phone when he clicks off the line.

I should call him back, but I don't. Why? I don't know. Why do panicked women do anything?

Ten minutes later, the phone rings again, and I am surprised by how much I want it to be Leo. It is.

"It's going to be all right, okay?" I hear his voice on my machine. "I just want you to know that. It's a gruesome script, but it'll be okay. No panicking, got it?"

I click on the phone that's been sitting on my lap. "How can you be sure?"

Leo sighs on the other end. "I suppose I'm not. But I thought it needed saying." After a pause he adds, "I hear things are crazy over at the studio. How are you?"

"I've always trusted Nigel to know how far to push things but…" I don't want to finish that sentence.

"Well," says Leo, with a sad excuse for a chuckle, "if Nigel wanted to get the network's attention, trust me, an animated prime-time suicide gets their full attention."

"Look, I'm not in favor of weasels offing themselves for entertainment value, but there's so much compassion in the aftermath that if we can just get Nigel to…"

"Lindy, don't." Leo's voice is soft and steady. "Don't pretend this isn't exactly what it is. It's hard enough without having to try and gloss over it."

"No, I'm not glossing. The suicide's got to go, but we can still stay edgy. We've made the network nervous before. Nigel will know it's time to pull back." I hate the doubt rising in my voice.

"Do you want me to come over there? Are you okay?"

"No." The answer shoots out of me. "I'm not okay, but don't come over here." I squint my eyes shut. "Ugh, I don't know what I want. I just don't think you being here would be a good idea right now."

"It's your call. I'll do what you want."

Want? Who knows what I want? "What are you going to do, Leo?"

"Well, right now I'm going to figure out

just how irked everybody is around here. Figure out who's mad and how much. It's too early for sponsors to get all itchy, so I'll just talk to as many people as I can. Sort of a damage assessment."

That sounds ominous. "Then?"

"Then," Leo replies with a sigh in his voice, "I'll think of all the things we can do about it and pick one."

He makes it sound so simple. "They'll listen to you, right?"

"Usually they do."

I sit up. "What do you mean, 'usually'?"

"Sometimes they've already made up their minds, and it doesn't matter what I tell them. It happens. I don't own the network, I just work for them. Remember that."

Definitely not what I wanted to hear. And then again, maybe it is. If Leo tells them to give *Arborville* another shot and they don't listen to him, it's not Leo's fault.

Maybe not, but I'm still out of a job. Out of the best job in the universe. Could it get more confusing? "Do you think we're goners, Leo?"

"Honestly, I don't know. The script's

way over the edge, but Nigel's pushed the boundaries before and gotten away clean. He's had better ratings before, though, so they've given him a longer leash in the past. They might rein him in tight, they might just give him enough rope to hang himself. Or they might just let someone else take over."

"You mean fire Nigel. Leo, you don't just fire a show's creator."

"It might happen."

"That'll kill us for sure."

"Lindy, you don't know that. Nigel's a talented guy, but he doesn't hold the monopoly on edgy wit. Believe it or not, there are other guys as good as Nigel out there."

"No, there aren't. You can't fire Nigel. Even for this."

"I might not have a choice. And it might not even be up to me."

"I can't stand this. You've got to do something."

Frustration rises in his voice. "How on earth did you survive in this business if you take things so personally? It's television. It's Nigel. Don't make this about me. And don't make this about us."

I'm pacing the room now. "What do you mean, 'don't make this about us'? How can this not be about us? This is all about us."

"No, it's about our jobs. There's a difference."

That's the network talking if ever I heard it. "Not to me! I love my job. I love the show. *Arborville* deserves to stay on the air. You said so yourself, nobody does it better than we do."

"That was true," Leo argues. Past tense.

I stop and glare at the phone. "That's a lousy thing to say, Leo."

"Can you please stop getting so emotional about this?" His voice is rising now, too. "You're making a bad situation worse. I'm not thrilled to be in this position, you know. I'm not enjoying this."

"Then fix it. You can do that. You said you wanted the power to keep the good stuff on the air, well, now you've got it. Use it. Nigel's being a jerk, but no one has to lose their jobs over it. It's one lousy script. One. Out of how many seasons of great stuff? You've got to fix this." I'm staring at my Emmy, suddenly getting the urge to shine it up.

"Don't turn this into some kind of test, Lindy."

"Well, it is, isn't it?" I'm stomping around the room now, flailing my arms as my anger rises. I'm not being careful about what I say anymore; the chips are going on the table. "Maybe not for you, though. You're safe, aren't you? You get to keep your job either way, so what's it matter to you? You'll either be the hero who saved *Arborville* or the man brave enough to bring it down. You'll be one step closer to your beloved power mongering. It's only me who can lose here, isn't that right?"

"You're way off base...I—"

I don't want to hear it. "Am I? Think about it, Leo. Let's play it your way and leave the personal part out of it. You're holding all the cards. Don't tell me not to get panicky. I have every right to be nervous."

"You don't have every right to take it out on me."

"Why not? You don't get to make me

fall for you and then be the guy to take my job away." Yikes! I did *not* mean to say that just now. I'm standing in the middle of my living room, cringing, and punching myself in the head. That is definitely not how I wanted this moment to go. There's a gaping silence on Leo's end of the phone. "Leo…say something."

"I'm coming over there."

"No!" I cry out, twirling around. "I'm a wreck already, don't make me botch this face-to-face when I've stuck my foot in my mouth over the phone."

"I see no botching. As a matter of fact, this conversation just took a definite turn for the better. You should see my smile at the moment."

"I just yelled at you."

"Yeah, but it's what you yelled that made all the difference. Let me come over there."

"No," I say, sinking to the floor next to my laundry basket. "I'm feeling way too naked at the…"

"Oh, *definitely* the wrong word to use right now…"

Okay, cringing harder now. "*Vulnera-*

ble. Way too *vulnerable* at the moment to do this face-to-face." I fish a towel out of the laundry basket next to me on the floor and put it over my head in self-loathing.

There's a rich warmth to Leo's voice as he says, "Are you always this crazy?"

"No," I say, remembering when I e-mailed him a similar question. Of course, he was being romantic, and I'm sitting on my floor under a bath towel. "You do this to me."

"I think I'm glad. Actually, I know I'm glad."

"Glad one of us is glad." How stupid a thing was that to say?

"Okay, I'll stay put. How about," he says slowly, "we just let this work thing play itself out until Thursday's taping? Nothing has to happen until then—and not even then. We've got at least a month before that show airs. A lot can happen between now and then."

"You know, I saw this moment going a whole lot differently in my head."

Leo's laughing now. "It's just fine. A little weird, but I think I'm learning to like it that way."

"I hate how weird it is."

"Well, you know what they say."

"And what do they say?"

At that he begins to sing the opening lines of "It's Not Easy Being Green."

Chapter Twenty-Two

Another owl?

This will go down as one of the worst weeks in *Arborville* history. The studio was a firestorm of tension and finger-pointing. Even the intern called in sick by Thursday morning. I don't blame her. Here, taping this script, is about the last place I want to be.

Jason's got two people in the studio with him—I'm guessing one is his agent and the other is probably his lawyer. He's still got a whole year left on his contract. He'll still get all the money coming to him, but no one can write dialogue or airtime for a weasel who's killed himself, can they? Osgood's promised him the chance to voice a new character, but none of that's helping.

Dylan's dead, and Jason's livid. It will come as no surprise to you that taping goes badly. Nigel isn't satisfied with anyone's performances, and he's been arguing constantly with Osgood in the control booth. We can't hear him in the sound booth, but there's more than enough body language to ensure the points are being made. People are mad at Osgood, too, because they blame him for letting Nigel get away with this. They blame Jason for acting like a jerk even though I'd say he's rather justified.

Worst of all, however, is the look on Leo's face as he's watching this fight unfold. I can't put my finger on it, but something's there in his eyes that wasn't there before. Actually, it's more like something's not there that was there before. I'm watching him, feeling the pit in my stomach grow deeper and deeper.

"Are you reading the script *at all*, Lindy?" Nigel barks through my earphones. "It *says* 'Get over here *George,*' not 'Get over here Dylan.' Dylan's dead, remember? It's the whole point of the script. Dylan's dead. Dead, dead, stiff-on-the-tracks-and-not-coming-back dead."

I've tried to feel okay about this script, but I just can't. My conscience won't let me. Nigel's crossed the line, and I don't know what to do about it. Certainly not can the show or fire Nigel, but I feel as if I should do something. I just don't know what. Until I do, I have little choice but to keep listening for God's direction, and get through the next twenty-four hours.

"Lindy, do you think you might want to bring your brain to work next week? *Ahem!* Would it be asking too much for you to consider paying attention?" Nigel's rolling his eyes, teenager style.

Yea, though I walk through the valley of the shadow of unemployment....

I love my job, I love my job, I love my job....

"And finally we're done with Miss Edwards. Sixty-seven takes in all, love, I do believe that's a record." Nigel scowls at me through bloodshot eyes. Usually, when Nigel gets like that, I see him with pity. Today, his eyes are so sharp and accusing that I feel no pity at all. I feel angry. Abused. As though I'm some sort of pawn in Nigel's larger-than-life-size chess set, stuck in a battle strategy I neither understand nor endorse.

"Well," I growl back as I yank the earphones off my head, "it's been a tough morning for all of us." I bang the earphones down hard enough to clang loudly in Nigel's ears.

I look up into the control booth, partly to catch Nigel's wince—and resultant dirty look—and partly in the hopes of seeing another banana shake offer floating in the air behind Nigel.

Leo's not even there. Somewhere in the bickering of the last half hour, he's left without anyone noticing.

My throat hurts, my head hurts and my stomach is twisted up like a sailor's knot. I need a shake, an aspirin and clear divine guidance—probably not in that order.

A quick check out my office window

reveals that Leo's car is not in the parking lot. That feels like bad news. Like he's gone off somewhere to gather his ammunition.

Then again, maybe the guy just has work to do. I mean, we can't be his only network project right now. There might be a cooking show that needs a new host selection. Soap operas needing new stars. Seven new reality shows to overmarket.

There's a Post-it note in Leo's handwriting stuck to my computer monitor. "I'll call you." He knows the show is on tonight, so he knows I'll be home watching it, so he's going to call. That's good. I am taking that as a good sign.

But I'm still going to Hogan's. I'm taking a short walk around the block first to pray again and preburn a few calories, but I'm banana-bound, that's for sure.

He's there, standing outside Hogan's.

No, not Leo. Worse.

Kyle is standing there outside Hogan's. I pray for direction from God and I get *Kyle?*

"Hey," he says, waving sheepishly. "They said I might find you here."

I stop in my tracks, feeling a bit, well, stalked. "Who said?"

"Some guy at the studio. I came looking for you earlier, but they said you were taping and that you'd probably stop by here later."

Is my addiction to posttaping banana shakes that well-known?

"You stopped by the studio?" I want to point out, incidentally, that this is a television no-no. If you work at a department store, or a coffee shop or the Eiffel Tower, people can stop by your work. You do not just "stop by" a studio. We have guards for that sort of thing.

Guards who, evidently, don't do their job very well.

Noting my look of mild shock, Kyle explains, "Well, they did give me a bit of a hard time at first, but then I explained that we were dating. They didn't believe me until some weird-looking guy came by the front desk and said he remembered my name from the flowers. So, even though they couldn't let me in, they told me you might be here."

Thanks, Nigel. You were already my favorite guy today.

"You okay?" Kyle's waving a hand in front of my face. "You look a little wired."

"Um…really bad day, that's all."

"At that job? You gotta be kidding me."

I choose not to take offense at that. I wondered, the other day, what I would feel like when I saw Kyle again. A twinge of regret, perhaps, a bit of swooning at those spectacular brown eyes.

Nope. I am standing here, completely swoon-free. Yes, he's attractive—I hadn't seen him in a suit before, and trust me, the guy cleans up *nice*. I think if I were a banker he'd even manage suave, but right now he looks all too starstruck.

"You'd be amazed, Kyle, what kind of bad day can happen at *Arborville*. It's just like any other job, just a little more public than most."

Kyle hikes back his suit jacket to put his hands in his pockets. Yes, Kyle could definitely do suave. "Well, then I guess I'd really better buy you that milk shake they said you'd come here for. Something about banana?"

Exactly how long did Kyle hang out at

the *Arborville* reception desk before someone realized he ought not to be there? Still, here is a guy just trying to be nice to me, and I've had a whole day of people being mean to me. Kyle's not a bad guy, just a guy who's a little too enamored of my job. I can live with that. Maybe God did send Kyle here as a distraction of sorts. "Who can resist an offer like that? Okay, let's eat."

As I slip into a booth, I wonder why on earth I just said yes. Kyle's like full-fat ice cream: feels great at first, but it can make you sick in large quantities and isn't good for you. Kyle fawns over me, and there's a part of me that really enjoys that. But he's not good for me. Get me fifteen minutes into a conversation with this guy, and he'll say something to remind me why I shouldn't get into a conversation with him again.

Am I making any sense?

Taking a deep breath, I attempt to set the record straight. "You know, I didn't think we *were* dating after that little escapade at your sister's house. Kyle, I thought we'd discussed this."

"Yeah, I know. I just didn't like ending it like that."

I give him points for that. We did end things badly, and I admire him for wanting to set things to rights. I order my milk shake, Kyle orders up a full lunch platter. "Shouldn't you be at work about now? It's the middle of the afternoon on Thursday."

"Sales managers get lunch hours, too, you know. Seriously, we have a client two blocks away. I never had the nerve to come to the studio before this, even though I knew it was close. Today, I found myself with a free couple of hours and thought I'd chance it."

Now might be a good time for a small education in media protocol. "It's not really a good thing to just show up at the studio, you know. They don't really like it. I'm amazed you got in at all without a pass." Actually, it's rather disturbing that he got in, but I chose not to share that just now.

"Just charm, I guess." He smiles, and I suddenly remember that our gate guard this morning was female. "Hey, was that weird guy I met—" Kyle makes a gesture representing a wild haircut "—the same Nigel who runs the show? The one who yelled from your phone?"

"Yep, that's our Nigel. We don't let him out into the real world much." I accept my beloved beverage. "You can see why." Cool, smooth bliss makes its way down my tender throat.

"I'd like to really meet him someday. Is he as crazy-wild-brilliant as he sounds?"

I have to chuckle at that one. "Oh, I think you've met all you want to of Nigel. He's better in small doses. And as for brilliant, well, I'd use a different word today."

Kyle tears into a BLT. "I still can't imagine," he says after considerable chewing, "that you can have a bad day at *that* job. For starters, it's two-thirty and you're done for the day."

"And you know, Kyle, that's the problem here." I am determined to get this straight once and for all. "I know you like the show. And I'm glad for that, really I am. But you've been a bit…hung up on it since you've known. That's not much fun for me."

"You've got to admit, it is cool."

"Okay, yes, it's cool." Hide the exasperation. Be friendly and considerate. "And it's good to be reminded that it's cool. I need that every now and then. But Kyle, do you realize you hooted after our first kiss?"

I think I'm relieved to see his surprise. "I did?"

"Granted, it was a great kiss…"

"It was, wasn't it?" He reaches for my hand. I all but swat him back.

"It was a mighty fine kiss, but hooting is not the reaction most women are looking for."

"Okay. So I won't hoot anymore."

Ugh! "That's not the point. The point is, I'm not sure you weren't more excited about kissing Maggie's voice than about kissing me." Can I get more direct than that?

"But you are Maggie's voice. I love the fact that you're Maggie's voice."

"Yes, yes, that much I know." He truly doesn't get it.

Do not, under any circumstances, ever let me say yes to any future meetings with this man. In another two conversations I might be taking out a restraining order. Will I ever learn?

"Besides," I continue, deciding on a more direct tactic, "you need to know there's someone else."

Kyle blinks at me. "Another owl?"

I feel lucky to have gotten out of lunch alive. Kyle may have turned me off banana shakes for life. I think I had to stop just short of "Go away and never talk to me ever again." I looked over my shoulder dozens of times on the drive home.

It's 8:45 p.m., the last fifteen minutes of *Arborville*'s weekly airing. It's a rerun— they call them "encore presentations," but you and I know what they really are—but they'll do that sometimes when we have an odd number of weeks in the season. This one's a classic. It's one of my favorite episodes from last season. Egyptian Woozy-Bird Flu has run through the forest, making people say what they really feel about each other. I've read this script twice, taped each line several times, watched it half a dozen times, and I'm *still* cracking up. That's the genius of *Arborville*—inside every bird is someone we know. I know someone who looks and acts like every character on the show—not because I know Nigel, but because *Nigel knows people*. Viewers in North Dakota are having the same reaction. Even viewers in England have the same reaction. Dylan Weasel just climbed up a tree to profess to Matilda Crow that if she'd just stop whining, she'd be the crow of his dreams. It's the first time Dylan and Matilda start their romance that fuels half of this past season's plot lines. Animals have been revealing loves, hates, secrets and crushes all over this episode, and it's simply hysterical.

I'm still giggling as I get up to answer my doorbell. If it's Kyle, I'm calling 9-1-1.

It's Leo.

He's wearing a pair of beat-up old khakis and the rain has soaked his bowling shirt. He looks awful.

"What happened to you? Are you okay?" I try to pull him in the door but he just stands there, his hair dripping onto his shoulders. "Get in here, you're going to be sick."

"No." His voice sounds like granite. Smooth and cold.

Now I'm just a little scared. "'No' what? Leo, what's going on?"

He looks at me, and the green of his eyes is almost dark and murky. All the clarity I saw there before is gone. "I'm going to cancel *Arborville*."

Chapter Twenty-Three

If Nigel stops pushing...

"I'm going to cancel *Arborville*." He can just blurt that out, as though it's a fact of life like gravity or mathematics?

Leo's going to ax *Arborville*. All the oxygen has just left the city of Los Angeles. I grab the doorway, feeling like a typhoon has just blown through my hall. I can't even form a reply. I can't even move.

Leo's staring into space, not even seeing me. "I went to an electronics store at eight o'clock tonight, and asked them to turn the televisions to *Arborville*. I sat there, watching the people in the store watch the show. People in the middle of buying washing machines stopped and laughed. Couples elbowed each other. It was brilliant."

I scrape some air into my lungs. "Leo, you're not making sense."

"No, no, that's just the point. It *was* brilliant. And it isn't anymore. *Arborville* isn't brilliant anymore. It's run its life-span."

"Don't say that. Brilliance isn't something that you use up like…like toothpaste."

Leo wipes the rain off his forehead but he still makes no move to come in my apartment. It's as if he's afraid to. "I've known it for weeks," he says, almost to himself. "I've seen it coming. But I just couldn't bring myself to do it." I feel his words sink through my body. "And tonight I realized I couldn't live with myself if I didn't," he continues. "It needs to go. Who am I if I don't face up to that?"

"You're the guy who's supposed to save us, that's who. The wonder man who's supposed to figure out how to keep the good stuff on the air, remember? There's still good stuff left in *Arborville!*"

"Not enough."

The somber resolve in his voice throws a match to the bonfire of panic that's been sitting in my stomach, just waiting to be lit. "Come on, there has to be another solution. Get new writers to work with Nigel. Okay, fire Nigel if you have to, but don't cancel the show. Don't let one bad script spell the end, Leo. Come in here, let me make some coffee," I begin tugging on his hand, which is disarmingly cold. "We'll figure out how to save it."

"No. I know the network. There's no figuring." At least he's walked into my living room. I'm not letting him out of this apartment until I get him to change his mind. I don't think he's told anyone yet so there's still time. "You were right about one thing, though," he says, almost offhandedly, as he wanders around my living room.

"What's that?"

"There is no *Arborville* without Nigel. I went back through the scripts that some of the other writers took the lead on, and they don't have the same edge. What makes Nigel great is the same thing that's going to take him off the air: he pushes. Pushes what we think, what we'll accept, what we assume, that sort of thing. If Nigel stops pushing, he stops being Nigel."

Leo has this rambling, shell-shocked quality about him that almost gives me the shivers. I don't like it. Leo needs to be in command to pull this off. Right now he looks anything but. I start pulling mugs out of the cupboard. Maybe I just need to keep him talking, keep his mind going until he finds the solution. "So let him keep pushing."

"The trouble with pushing, is that eventually you push too far." He makes eye contact with me from the kitchen door. It's the first time he's looked at me since he came in. "Come on, Lindy, you can't tell me you haven't seen it. The guy's a walking time bomb." Leo's voice begins to pick up speed. "He's on the verge of self-destruction. This week's script isn't the end of it, it'll just keep coming." He steps inside the kitchen, planting his hands on the kitchen island as he did on my desk that day.

I see it: he's made up his mind.

"Baloney," I counter. "It's 'kept coming'

for four years. I've heard the 'he's gone too far this time, it'll blow up in his face soon' speech *every one* of those four years." I tear the first coffee filter I get out of the box, and squelch the urge to ball it up and throw it at Leo. I stuff the second one into the machine. "Every year Nigel comes out with a script that is more tender, more poignant. We've had two shows this year with glimmers of faith. Can't you see? There's still far more right about *Arborville* than this one wrong script. And up until now we've been milder than some of what's out there. Than *lots* of what's out there." I turn and glare at him. "You can't tell me *you* don't know *that.*"

Leo grabs his hair with his hands, blowing out an exasperated shot of air. "We've had this argument before. Twice. I've got to look at where *Arborville* is headed. That's my *job.*"

"Don't *you* forget this is my job we're talking about. Don't you forget that if you do this, I'm out of a job and you aren't." I rip the lid off the coffee can.

Leo groans, bangs his hand on the

counter and disappears back into the living room. I plunge the scoop into the grounds and dump them into the coffeemaker. "Okay, fine. Forget the network for a moment," he practically yells from the living room. Then he appears in the kitchen doorway again. "Think about you. You're a person of faith. You can't tell me you haven't wondered if Nigel's crossed the line from just shocking to immoral. Violence for entertainment is wrong. You know he'll go further. You *know* he will. What happens when Nigel decides to take on the church? When he writes an episode with a murder in it? Child abuse? Can you stand by then?"

I slam down the coffee can. "So you're canceling *Arborville* for me? Don't save me from myself, Leo. I'm a big girl."

"No, that's not what I'm saying. I'm just trying to get you to think about…"

"*Arborville is* my stand, Leo. I'm not happy now, sure, but I'm not going to throw my hands up and walk away. That's not the only other option here. Have you even tried to come up with another solution? You're—" I stick both hands in the air, making those annoying quotation gestures with my fingers "—'The Save Guy.' Well, think of all the good *Arborville*'s done and save it. Or isn't that part of your job anymore?"

In a sick, twisted detail, the *Arborville* closing theme song lilts out from my television. For a moment we both stop, listening. *Oh, Lord Jesus, help! This is so awful. Leo's squinting his eyes shut, as if it hurts to hear the music, and I wonder if he's yelping out the same cry of help to you, Lord.*

"*Arborville* doesn't have to die yet," I say, not caring that it sounds like pleading. "Don't be the man who kills it." I realize, at that moment, that as much as I don't want *Arborville* to end, it's just as painful to me that Leo would be the man to bring that end about. Leo's condemnation, even if it isn't the ax, is handing the network the ax. Networks know what do to with axes— no one has to tell them.

Leo stabs a finger at me. "I'm not the one killing *Arborville*, Lindy. Nigel is doing that all on his own."

I push away the tiny possibility that Leo may be right. I won't go there. It's too convenient to blame the eccentric, uncontrollable artistic guy. Artistic guys don't come any other way. That's why there are producers. Leo seems twice as smart as Evan Osgood, and Osgood's been handling Nigel for years. "You are," I blurt out. "You know you are. You just can't own up to it. Leo Corbin has finally met the show he can't save. How does *that* truth feel?"

"You know," Leo bellows, his voice dark and dangerous, "I came tonight because I thought you deserved to be the first to know. That we deserved the chance to work this out. Together. I was a fool. I don't know why I thought this was a good idea." Leo jerks my door open. "I hope you're decent enough to keep this between us. I trusted you with this information. Don't make me a bigger fool by using it."

Without another word, Leo storms out into the hallway, slamming my door shut behind him.

It seems to make the whole world shudder in his wake.

Chapter Twenty-Four

Do or die

Lecture me all you want on ethics, but if Nigel's the one killing *Arborville,* then he's the one who can save it. Especially if Leo won't. So I don't want to know whether or not you approve of the fact that I'm in my car, heading over to Nigel's apartment. No more quiet listening. It's do-or-die time, and I'm in no mood to die.

Nigel answers after four rings. "I hadn't expected to see you on my doorstep. What's the matter? Your friend not find you for lunch?"

Friend? Oh, that's right, I have Nigel

to thank for my lovely encounter with Kyle. "Kyle? He's the least of my worries. Let me in."

"Couldn't you have rung up or something? I've got…company."

"Hi." A wispy woman, sporting spiky, near-white hair and black eye shadow, peers over Nigel's shoulder. "Ooo," she coos in a woozy soprano, "you must be Lindy. The owl's voice, right? You had a fight with Nigel this morning and now you've come over to make up, huh?"

I recount my troubles to my journal or my Lord. Nigel, it seems, prefers an endless stream of vapid blondes for retrospection. "No." I make it as curt and urgent as a single syllable can sound.

Nigel's peeling what's-her-name's hand off his chest. "Can't it wait till tomorrow?"

"No." I give Nigel a "don't make me say it a third time" glare. "This needs to be now, Nigel. Right now."

Nigel sighs. "Tiff, love, I'm in the mood for sushi. How about you run and get us some while Lindy and I clear up whatever this is. We'll pick up where we left off—"

he punctuates that with a sloppy kiss that makes me cringe "—when you get back. Be a good love and get me some tuna and the bitty rolls with the crab in them, got it?" He peels three twenty dollar bills— way too much for what he just ordered— and threads them in between the black nail polish of her fingers. Chuckling, he swats at her as she bounces out the door.

There are days when Nigel really tries my patience. When I'm tempted to give up on him ever being a healthy contribution to the human race. Today, however much he grosses me out, doesn't get to be one of those days. Nigel's artistic weirdness is the thing that can save us—I don't get to quibble about the regrettable side effects.

"All-righty, you've got me undivided attention." Nigel plops down on his white leather couch and sits cross-legged. "Have at it." He pats the cushion next to him.

I prefer to deliver this standing. "Leo Corbin's going to cancel *Arborville.* Tomorrow, probably. And after that fiasco of a taping today, if we don't do something about it, we're going to be out of jobs."

Nigel's gears are spinning to take it all in. "Corbin? Mr. Network Nasty?"

"Mr. Network Nasty happens to have a lot of clout and we certainly showed him our best side this week, didn't we?"

"Oh, come off it, love." Nigel picks up a glass of whatever he was drinking, inspects it briefly, then downs it. "We've had those blokes breathing down our backs before this and come out fine." The instant frog in his throat lets me know that whatever's in that glass is nothing he needs more of right now. I snatch it and the bottle next to it and put them on the counter behind me.

"No need to get all— Hey, how do you know all this, anyway? How come you know first?" His eyebrows push down into a suspicious glare.

"Because he just came over to my apartment and told me, that's why. Who cares how I know? I know, and now you know. You've finally gone too far. So *do something* before you find yourself writing game show questions for union scale." Nigel's blank look tells me I'm not getting through the alcohol haze. "Did you hear me? We're about to get axed. You want to keep your job or what?"

His face finally registers the jolt. I've gotten his attention. He stands up and starts pacing the room. *Thank you, Lord. I needed to get through to him. Now we stand a chance.*

Nigel stops and stares at me. "He fancies you. That's it. I've seen it for weeks, and not put it together. You've been seeing him. Got it for you, does he?"

I do not, not, *not* want to get into this now. "Nigel…"

"How else would he know where you live? And he's always in your office. And you. You fancy him. It's all over your face. You've had a grin about you. All along I thought it was Mr. Flowers—who only really fancies Maggie, you know—and here it was our little network spy!" He points at me. "You've been sleeping with the enemy!"

"I have *not* been sleeping with anyone, Nigel, stop it. Can we just focus on the fact that we're about to lose our jobs here for a moment?"

"Oh, you've got it for him. And now he's made you mad by axing the show and you want to get even." He starts pacing again, waving his arms around. "Fine, so let's call in Nigel. He's brilliant. He'll write us a script everyone will just die for, and we'll all be saved." He whirls around to point another dramatic finger at me, but he's too drunk to pull it off without wobbling like a toy, bumping soundly into his glass dining room table and setting the candlesticks rocking. "Can't you all see I've already given you the script to die for? We're going where no show has gone before. 'Boldly' or whatever that space captain says."

I sigh. "The only person dying for that script is Jason, and that's because you killed him off. You killed off the favorite character. What were you thinking?"

"I'm *visioning*. I'm exploring how everyone copes with the loss of their favorite scapegoat." He adopts a swooning pose. "What will everyone do without Dylan Weasel around? Who will they blame? What's life like without the resident bad guy?"

Why did I think coming here would help? "Nigel, will you *sit down?*"

Nigel sits down and hugs his knees to his chest. He pops his chin onto his knees and stares at me like some nocturnal creature with spiked hair. "So, do you love him?"

"No!"

"Ooo, way too quick an answer. Hate's not the opposite of love, you know. Very close emotions, those two. You can hate someone you love."

Speaking of hating someone...

I take a deep breath and insert as much calm as humanly possible into my voice. "We went out a few times, but as of this evening things are definitely off. Can we talk about the show, Nigel? Can you focus for *just a minute?*"

"Did he come over to tell you how much he struggled with his decision? How it broke his heart to can our show?" Nigel bats his eyes and clutches his heart. "How it hurts him more than it hurts you?"

Words cannot express how much I don't want to get into this. Not now, and certainly not with Nigel. "You've got to write a new script. You've got dozens in your head, I know you do. Write a new one. You can do that. You're that good."

"But I *like* this script."

I feel as if I'm dealing with a five-year-old. "Do you like your job? Do you think you'll still have one when Leo gets through with us?"

"Ooo, it's *Leo* now, is it? How do we know anyone's going to listen to Leo anyway?"

The urge to scream burns in my throat. "They're going to listen to him because you keep handing them reasons to!" My shouting brings Marilyn sauntering out of her tropics to see what's going on. She sways across the floor like a miniature alligator, feet creeping in opposing pairs across the white carpet. She looks at me, looks at Nigel, then ambles over to his feet. He picks her up and strokes her slowly, looking like the evil scientist with the white cat in all those James Bond movies.

"I think you love him. He's gotten under your little control-freak skin and you can't stand it. What's our little Lindy going to do now?"

"Okay, I liked him a lot, but Nigel, *he's canceling the show!* Are you not listening to me?"

"We're bigger than he is. He can't hurt us." He addresses his remarks to Marilyn.

"It doesn't matter what you think Leo can and can't do. Nigel. *Nigel!* Listen to me!" I'd take Nigel's face in my hands if I thought that would help. Instead, I stare straight into his red-rimmed eyes. "Leo's going to cancel *Arborville!*"

"It won't happen. They won't listen to him."

"They'll listen to him."

"Why? Because you love him?"

"Will you *stop* that? They'll listen to him because he's right, do you hear me? If you keep pulling scripts like this week, you give them dozens of reasons to cancel *Arborville.*" I sink into one of the dining table chairs across from him. "What's the matter with you? This script was ugly. Ugly. Not edgy or brilliant or any of those adjectives you love to use. It was gross, Nigel. Not one person liked it." I catch my breath. "I love everything you do, I've loved everything you've written. Even when you make me squirm, even when I think you're wrong, I love your talent. You make me *think*. But this one…wake up, Nigel, you've gone too far."

For a flicker of a moment, I see it registering. See a glint of sadness behind all that defiance. Maybe, just maybe, I've gotten through. Then, *poof,* it's gone, and the "I dare you" face is back. "You know, love, I always thought you were the one person who understood me best. But you don't get it, either, do you? I haven't gone too far. I haven't even really started. There's loads more where that came from."

I left. There wasn't anything else to do.

Driving home, it hits me so hard I have to pull the car over.

I sit there, on the edge of the street, and sob into my steering wheel. I rant and rave and curse Nigel and his stubborn, brilliant, defiant, annoying…

…truth.

I am in love with Leo.

I'm angry that *Arborville* is in jeopardy,

but I'm even angrier that I'm in love with the man who made it happen. I fell in love with him back there, at the restaurant, when I saw his vision for the world. I fell for the man on a quest. I fell for the man who had to cancel *Arborville* because that's who he is.

Nigel *has* been handing the network reasons to cancel the show. He will keep going farther and farther over the edge. I just didn't want to see it. Nigel's lost his touch. I never thought that could happen, and I didn't want to hear it from anyone, least of all Leo. I didn't want him to be right, but that doesn't change the fact that he is. I think I fell for him because he saw what's right, even before I knew what it was.

I fell for the man who would come over to my apartment and tell me he's going to take away from me the thing I love most.

The thing I love the most.

Oh, Father, forgive me. My heart splits open to a fissure so deep and dark I can hardly bear it. *When did* Arborville *become the thing I love the most?*

Chapter Twenty-Five

Why the men's room has a dead bolt

I've tried Leo's PDA, his cell phone, his office number and his e-mail. Nothing.

Great. I finally figure out I love the guy and he drops off the planet. *Come on, Lord, You can do better than this. You like happy endings, too, don't You?*

I'm pacing my apartment, pulling my hair out, stumped. It's only eleven-thirty and this is Los Angeles. One woman ought to be able to locate one guy. Do I know anyone on the police force? Can you send out an APB for purely romantic reasons?

I could have Suz put it out over the air.

Nope, she's not on. Who knows if Leo's anywhere near a radio, anyway. With my luck I'd have six guys claiming to be Leo Corbin phoning me within the hour.

I'm pacing so wildly I step right into the end of a knitting needle. The one protruding from my infamous green-and-brown sweater. The one I actually thought would guide me. *Lord,* I shoot up the twentieth confession of the night. *I botched all of this up so badly, it's a wonder You didn't give up on me. I was foolish beyond foolish, wasn't I? Please, don't let me lose it all now. Give me the chance to get things straight before you pull the rug out from underneath me. I don't care how it goes down tomorrow at work, we'll get to that soon enough. Just let me find Leo now. Don't let him go through tomorrow without knowing what he needs to know. What I need him to know.*

What did he say he did when he was angry? Clean his car? Great, it's raining. There goes that option. Where *is he?* I'm going to find him, somehow. I reach into the closet for my raincoat. My foot stubs into the box that holds the bowling ball Leo gave me. *Of course!*

I know where Leo is. Except it's closing in half an hour, and I'm not sure I can make it there in time. Inspired, I call information and ask for the phone number of Ten Pin Alley. Gratitude swells in my heart when I hear Dino's voice answer.

"Dino, it's Lindy. You remember, Lindy?"

"Leo's girl?"

Okay, not my favorite way to put it but it's no night to be picky. "Yeah, Leo's girl. Please, please tell me he's there."

"Oh, he's here all right. Been slamming pins down for a couple of hours. What'd you do to make him so mad?"

"I'd rather not go into it right now, but could you do me a favor?"

"What?"

"Keep him there. Just keep him there till I get there, okay?"

There's a pause on the other end. "I don't know. He's pretty mad and we close at midnight."

"Please, Dino, I'm begging you."

"Oh, I'll do it all right, I just didn't know

if you wanted me to tie him down or something. He's real mad and I'd sort of want your permission in case it gets ugly or somethin'."

I don't know whether to laugh or worry. "You have my complete permission to do whatever it takes to keep Leo there. Whatever it takes."

"You mean that?"

"With every bone in my body. I'll be there in half an hour. Sit on him if you have to."

"You got it, missy."

Here we go, Lord. Just You and me and twenty minutes to Ten Pin. Can you fix the traffic lights for me? Part the red sea of L.A. traffic? Or at least just help me say the right thing once I get there?

My tires squeal into the parking lot at Ten Pin alley twenty-three minutes later at 12:10. It's still raining lightly, but I don't care at all. I run out of my car and blast through the doors to find...no one.

Oh, no.

Then I hear it. Bangs. Leo's voice, muffled, angry, from somewhere off to my left. I go racing through the back lobby to find Dino, sitting on a chair leaned back against the men's room door. His chair is shaking a bit with each bang on the door behind it. Silently grinning, he points to the thrown dead bolt on the upper right hand corner of the door.

"Dino! I'm stuck in the bathroom! Some idiot threw the drunk lock on the door and I'm in here! Diiinnnooo!"

"The drunk lock?" I mouth to Dino.

"It's how we keep guys under control until the police get here when things get out of hand. Works great, don't it?"

"Dino! Man, I thought you'd left. Get me out of here." Leo's voice comes from behind the scratched, grimy door.

"Safer than tying a big angry lug like him down or something, too."

"Who on earth are you talking to out there? Dino!" Three more bangs jostle Dino and his chair.

"You want I should let him out now?" He crosses his hands over his chest and cocks his head to one side.

"I think it'd be best for all concerned, don't you?"

All motion stills on the other side of the door.

"That'd be your call, missy. He didn't sound too safe a minute ago. 'Course, I figured it'd be much more fun if I didn't tell him why I was locking him up."

"Dino, who knew you were a romantic?"

"*You* locked me in here?" comes Leo's voice, accompanied by a whopping bang on the door that nearly sends Dino's chair over. "Lindy? Is that you? What is going on out there?"

A huge grin breaks across Dino's salt-and-pepper whiskers. "Guilty."

"Get me out of here *now!*" booms Leo from behind the door.

"Easy there, big fella. I'm unlockin' the door now." He waves me back a few paces and I comply. "Now, don't do nothin' stupid." Dino picks up the plastic chair with one hand while he flips the dead bolt over with the other, then sidesteps the door as it flies open.

Leo takes two huge steps into the lobby, and stares at me. I can't for the life of me read his expression. It's everything—anger, confusion, surprise, worry, pleasure—all at once. My heart does a flip in my chest. Now would be a good time to say something clever, but I'm drawing a complete blank. Come on, Lindy, major moment in the works here, don't choke.

Serious choke. I can't find a single word to say.

Dino clears his throat.

Leo wipes his hands down his face, trying to make sense of the last twenty minutes. "Anyone want to tell me what's going on here?"

"Well, she calls me askin' if you was here…"

"Dino," I interrupt, deciding I'd better say anything I can rather than let Dino relate things, "could you…um…give us a moment?"

"Sure," he grins, and attempts a wink. It looks wildly out of place on his tough-guy features, "I gotta go clean somethin'. Lock up. That sort of thing."

Leo stuff his hands in his pockets. I twist my coattail up in my hands. Ten minutes ago

I was bursting to get these words out, but now that I'm standing here, I'm terrified.

"How about you tell me—" he starts.

"Do you love me?" I blurt out. I have never needed to know anything more than I need to know this one thing right now.

His eyes widen.

"Do you love me?" I can't stand the quiet. "Because I just realized I'm in love with you and I don't think I can do this if I'm in it alone and I really need to—"

Leo silences me with a kiss that makes the world tilt. Suddenly I'm in his arms and they hold the whole world up around us. It's as if time is boiled down to this one perfect moment where I melt against him. Exquisite. Breathless. And suddenly we're laughing, and his hands are running through my wet hair and holding my forehead close to his while he says, "Yes. Yes, Lindy, I am in love with you. Yes, affirmative, you betcha, definitely…"

"Got it." I say. I throw my arms around him and kiss him again, standing up on my toes. Leo grabs me by the waist and spins me around. It's just like the movies. Only it's real, here, now. "Wow."

"Yeah, that about covers it," Leo says against my neck. "Wow." He sets me down gently, but doesn't take his hands off my waist. "Want to tell me what happened?"

I relate my conversation with Nigel. As I tell the story, I suddenly realize the arguments I gave to Nigel were the same arguments Leo gave to me. I just wouldn't listen to them until I saw, for myself, how far Nigel had sunk. I'd put my faith in Nigel's unfailing talent, only to wake up and realize Nigel's talent was fallible. Nigel's only human. Come to think of it, Nigel's barely human.

Another confession, Lord. How did my trust get so misdirected without my even realizing it?

"You told Nigel I was going to recommend cancellation?" We slip into one of the restaurant booths. Leo is not pleased.

Yet another confession. "I know you asked me not to. I'm sorry. I was so angry and so sure Nigel would do something to save the show."

Leo takes a deep breath and rubs his eyes. "That was a really bad idea. How'd he take it?"

"He's Nigel. He ranted and raved and dared you to take him down in all his brilliance."

"He got angry did he? That's good."

"Not for me it wasn't. He'd already had half a bottle of something before I even got to him. You know Nigel—it's all high drama even without the booze."

"But he was okay when you left?"

"I didn't stick around long enough to take his temperature. He was banging things around, saying we 'hadn't seen anything yet.' Classic Nigel tantrum behavior. I left."

"You left him alone."

"Yes, he's a grown up—okay, barely—I didn't feel like I ought to call a sitter. Besides, he had a date there when I got there. He sent her out for sushi, so she was going to be back soon. What are you getting at, Leo?"

Leo draws his hands down his face again. "People sometimes do stupid things when shows get canceled. We've seen it before. We actually plan for it. Some people really go off the deep end when they find out. Especially the Nigel types."

I look at him. "Oh, come on, it's not that bad, is it?"

"No offense, but look at you. You didn't exactly haul off and be reasonable now, did you? It's like being fired. Sometimes that's the last straw in someone's composure and things get ugly."

"And you're worried Nigel will get ugly?"

Leo leans his elbows on the table. "Aren't you?"

I'm fishing in my purse for my cell phone to call Nigel when it rings in my hands. Nigel's cell comes up on my screen. "It's Nigel," I call to Leo over my shoulder. Things must be okay.

"Hello?"

A shrill woman's voice comes over the receiver. "Is this Lindy? Did I reach Lindy?"

"Yes. Who is this?"

"Tiffany. Oh, great, look at him. Oh, man."

"Tiffany who? Where's Nigel?" I wave Leo over from changing his shoes.

"You know, Tiffany! We met when you came over. I just clicked around till I found your name on his cell phone. He's out, man, out cold. He did something. I couldn't think of what else to do."

My spine ices over. "What do you mean he's 'out'? Tiffany, tell me what's going on."

"I got sushi and it took awhile, you know?"

Yes, I'm thinking, with forty extra bucks I bet it took you awhile.

"And when I got back, he didn't answer the door quick, but when he did he was all droopy and sloshed out of his mind."

"So Nigel was drinking." No real surprise there.

"Yeah, and I didn't think much of it until I found the pills on the couch."

My heart drops through the floor. "Pills?"

Leo freezes.

Chapter Twenty-Six

Scary concepts

"A whole bunch of perco-somethings," Tiffany whimpers into the phone. "He must've taken a dozen of these. Now he's out cold. He don't look good at all. You think I should call a doctor or something?"

"I think you should call an ambulance. Now. Hang up and call an ambulance." Just to be safe, I add, "Call 9-1-1, that's how you call an ambulance, okay? 9-1-1."

"I just found another bottle of something else on the kitchen table." She gasps. "It's empty." Her voice sounds on the verge of tears. I'm not far behind myself.

"Tiffany, listen to me. Keep both those bottles and show them to the paramedics when they get there. And find the bottle of whatever he was drinking—find the glass if you can. Hang up now and call 9-1-1. I'm on my way, okay?"

"I don't wanna do this."

"No one wants to do this. But you're there. Now stop talking to me and call 9-1-1. Right now. We'll be there in no time."

I feel Leo's hand on my shoulder, and it destroys any hope I have of keeping tears at bay. "Leo…"

He pulls my hand. "Tell me in the car. We'll take mine so you can make calls on the way."

I'm nearly tripping as we head out the door at a run. "We gotta save him, Leo."

"Hey," he says, punching the unlock button on his keys and dashing around to the driver's side. "I'm the 'save guy' remember?" We get in and he roars the engine to life. "Take a deep breath. You can go to pieces in an hour, but right now Nigel needs you. Do you have Osgood's home number?"

I dial while Leo prays aloud. His voice is urgent and pleading as he asks God to send the paramedics, to give them wisdom and to keep Tiffany calm enough to help. Osgood's voice mail kicks in. "Voice mail."

"Hang up and try again." Leo says, taking a turn a little faster than legal. "He probably didn't wake up fast enough to catch the phone."

I look at my watch. How did it get to be 1:05 already? I hit Redial, and this time Osgood picks up. When I give him the ten-second rundown, he tells me which hospital to head for. Then he admits that he's done this once before with Nigel.

Nigel's tried something like this before? And I didn't know? *Lord, I plead, he's worse than I thought. Don't let him go, not yet. Give him a third chance to find You.*

Twenty-five agonizing minutes and four phone calls later, Leo's tires screech into a parking place at the hospital. We both run toward the E.R. doors. Osgood's there, looking dazed and rumpled. He's pacing around the floor, his gangly frame looking as though he is suspended from a sharp hook between his shoulder blades. He looks up from his cell phone to stare at Leo.

"Corbin?"

"Later," I intercept. No point right now in launching the complicated explanation of why I'm chatting with the network exec at one in the morning. "Where's Nigel?"

"They're in pumping his stomach now. He's a mess, and they won't tell me much, but no one's looking panicked yet. Except for Nigel's date—she bolted out of here like a rabbit the minute she saw someone else was around. She looked all of nineteen—probably afraid of getting caught for something."

"Can we see him? His doctors?"

"Not now. And maybe not soon. All that 'immediate family only' business."

"We *are* Nigel's immediate family. Anyone else is in England. I mean, come on, it's already *noon* there. He needs someone in with him *now!*" I turn to the commando-faced nurse behind the counter. "He shouldn't be alone right now, somebody should be in there with him."

"He's having *a procedure*," she replies

curtly. "I wouldn't let his own mother in there with him right now. Until he's coherent enough to ask for one of you, you're just going to have to wait for the doctors to do their job."

"Osgood…" I give him my "do something!" glare.

"I've already tried, Lindy. We've just got to wait this one out."

"But…"

"I'll just take Lindy for a walk," Leo interjects, grasping my arm. "Call her cell if anything changes?"

Osgood stares hard at Leo. "Okay," he says slowly, a dozen questions in his eyes.

"I don't need a cup of coffee. We should go back in case…"

"Just come with me, will you? I know something we can do." Leo pulls me down the hallway to the directory, stares at it for a moment, then pulls me down two more hallways. Finally, he takes my hand as he pushes open the hospital chapel doors. It's bathed in quiet. A half-dozen candles flicker in one corner. Without a word, we walk hand in hand up to the front and sit down.

Leo takes my other hand and bows his head. My entire body feels as if it's deflating, melting off its desperate bones, as I bow mine. *"Father,"* Leo prays, his voice filled with all the strength I no longer posses, *"Nigel needs Your mercy. He needs Your protection and Your grace. We feel helpless right now. We don't want this to be the end."* Leo is giving voice to everything I cannot say. It feels as if he's pried open my heart and is reaching inside it, drawing it out before God. I'm awed and grateful. *"Save Nigel from his own desperate act,"* Leo continues, and I feel my heart echo his words. *"Save him because Lindy cares so much about what happens to him. Spare him. He's got so much talent. But he's so troubled. Forgive him."*

Leo is quiet for a moment. Even with my eyes shut and my soul reeling, I feel his gaze. I open my eyes to see him looking up toward me. "Forgive *me,* Lindy," he nearly whispers. "I couldn't save *Arborville.* I couldn't save Nigel."

I had not, until this moment, realized what it cost Leo to cancel *Arborville.* What it will cost Leo if Nigel doesn't pull through. To know he delivered the blow that proved one blow too many. Right now, in Leo's eyes, I see the defeat of a man who tried every solution he could think of until the truth would have it no other way.

Leo canceled *Arborville* because *Arborville* had to be canceled.

Then it dawns on me. "You knew the show wasn't going to make it weeks ago, didn't you?"

His hands tighten on mine. "Actually, the decision came down before we even met. The network had decided this would be *Arborville*'s last season back in December. I wouldn't go along with it. I asked for the chance to come here because I thought there was a way to keep *Arborville* on the air. I came here to fight the cancellation, not to make it happen. And I failed."

I don't know what to say. There I was, thinking Leo's the guy trying to bring us down, and he's the guy fighting to save us. He came to my apartment tonight, admitting his defeat, and I tossed him out on his ear for being an incompetent coward. I deserve the Emmy for Most Complete Fool. "Thank you," I choke out, "for trying." I reach out and brush a wave of his hair off his forehead. I gaze into the depths of those green eyes, and know, down to my toes, that I love this man. Not for how he looks, or how well he kisses or how well he bowls, but for who he is. "Why didn't you ever tell me?"

"I suppose I tried to, a dozen times. But things always got tangled up. Then I started to have doubts about whether I could pull it off. Things kept getting worse, and I didn't want to face the fact that the first show I couldn't save was the one I wanted to save most of all." Leo pulls me into the crook of his arm, and for the only time tonight I feel safe. Suddenly exhausted, I let my head fall onto his shoulder. He kisses my forehead and sighs. "Then there was you. From the moment you told me off in your office, I couldn't get you out of my mind. You kept complicating things. Getting under my skin."

"Yeah," I say, threading my fingers through his, "I'm like that."

"Before I knew it I was saving *Arborville* for you as much as for my undefeated record. Then mostly for you. You know, be heroic and all that stuff. Make you like me. I kept trying to convince myself that it would be okay, that I'd save the day and we'd ride off into the sunset."

"Then?"

"Then when I began to realize I couldn't save the day, the thought of you hating me for it scared me to death. I'm not usually like this. I'm the guy in control. Suddenly some tiny brunette with a great voice is calling all the shots and I'm in full-fledged panic mode."

"I wasn't exactly cordial and diplomatic about this, was I?"

"You love your job. You love the people here. And…well…you're a bit of a control freak, you know."

I turn my eyes up toward him at that last remark.

"Hey," he defends himself, "takes one to know one." Leo breaks into a smile. "Control freaks in love. Hmm. Very scary concept." He pulls my head back down on his shoulder. The room holds a blanketing silence. The smell of candle wax mingles with the scent of Leo's leather jacket against my cheek. I feel his chest rise and fall with a deep breath. "We'll just have to ride this wave out."

"I don't suppose you surf as well as you bowl?"

"Nope," he sighs, kissing the top of my forehead again, "Never surfed at all."

I'm practically nodding off from sheer exhaustion when my cell phone rings.

"Lindy, Nigel's awake." Osgood sounds tired and annoyed. "And he's asking for you."

Chapter Twenty-Seven

The dumb and important question

You know, I thought I'd seen Nigel at his worst.

His present state, however, pretty much tops them all. The worst thing about it is how sad and small he looks. I've seen Nigel at his larger-than-life eccentric darkest, but this pale, broken-looking man makes my heart ache. I choke on a sob the minute he turns his head in my direction.

"Nigel, why?" It seems both the dumbest and the most important question right now.

"Dunno, really." His voice is like an echo of his usual voice. No edge, no volume and barely any emotion. "Just didn't want to be Nigel anymore, I suppose."

"The world needs Nigel Langdon around. I need you around." I grab his hand, disturbed at how limp it hangs in mine.

"Need's a funny thing, ain't it? We hardly ever want what we need, or need what we want."

I know Who you need, I think to myself, *I just wish you'd want Him.*

"You know," Nigel says, his head rolling slowly to one side as if all the alcohol hasn't quite left him yet, "I didn't even catch on."

"Catch on to what?"

"I didn't even realize I loved you till I realized you loved him. Funny, hmm?"

"Oh, Nigel." What do you say to something like that?

"Then suddenly, I'm sitting in my lovely apartment on my lovely couch and it pops into my head that I don't have anything I want. No show, no girl, my family's halfway across the world and they don't even ring me up anymore, and I can't think of a single thing to do with the rest of my life. Peaked at twenty-nine. Washed up.

My place in history will probably be as an entertainment question in future editions of Trivial Pursuit."

"Don't." I stroke his hand. "You've given the world *Arborville*. For years. Don't say that's nothing. Don't say that's all you've got."

"I don't have you, now, do I?"

"Of course you have me."

He cracks a melancholy smile. "So you'll leave Leo and take up with me, then?"

I kiss his hand. The whole thing seems so unbearably sad. I hope love makes far more sense in heaven—we've certainly made a first-class mess of it down here. "No, I won't." I can't lie to Nigel. I never could. And yet, the ache of not being able to give him the answer he'd like, to make all this go away and pull off a happy ending…it catches hard and choking in my throat. "I can tell you one thing. There'll always, *always* be a bag of cheese curls with our name on it."

"Cheese curls." Nigel's eyes flutter closed for a moment. "I loved those nights."

"I loved those nights, too. I think even God loved those nights, Nigel."

"I knew," he chuckles softly until he winces and starts coughing, "you'd say something like that."

"Are you okay?"

He opens one eye and glares at me, sparks of the old Nigel shining through the pale fog. "Well, that's a brilliant question given the circumstances, ain't it?"

"Can I…can I pray for you, Nigel?" I've asked him a dozen times before, and he's always said no. Surely, tonight will be different.

"No."

What is it going to take to get through to this man? "Well, why on earth not, you stupid, foolish man?" If I thought it wouldn't hurt so much, I'd take him by the shoulders and shake him.

"Because," he says, squeezing my hand, "I think it's about time I start praying for meself, don't you think?"

The crowd in The Soul Bowl at 3:30 a.m. is an interesting one. There are a few cops evidently too cool for the stereotypical doughnut shop, some blackleathered kids barely out of their teens who've obviously been out clubbing all night on Dad's credit card, a few people who look as if they're spending their last dime on a bowl of shredded wheat, and us.

Leo and Lindy. Ugh…doesn't it just sound awful, like a bad sitcom title? We're doomed as a couple. Leonard and Melinda sounds even worse. This is going to take some getting used to.

Tonight, the whole world takes getting used to.

"I haven't been up this late since…well, in a long time." I'm yawning into my yogurt and granola as I say it. Leo is on his second bowl of Cap'n Crunch, having evidently skipped dinner in the trauma of his network decision. "It's weird in here this time of night."

"This is L.A." Leo replies, cocking his head toward the woman in knee socks, a plaid skirt and pink hair two booths over. "Weird is standard operating mode. And it's this time of *morning,* by the way. I have to go to work in four hours."

Four hours. My trauma is winding down

a bit, but Leo's is just starting. Later today Leo has to agree to canceling *Arborville*. To formally admit that he couldn't save the show. To the people who were ready to can it in the first place. Leo is not a man who wears defeat well.

"I'm sorry. I mean, I'm sorry you have to do what you have to do." I wish I could come up with a more eloquent way to say what I'm feeling. "What do you think will happen?"

"Actually, it won't be that big a deal. I'll be reporting in alongside six or seven other network types who've been out assessing other projects. It'll be a four-minute discussion, tops. You'd be amazed how blasé these guys can be about uprooting sixty or seventy people's careers."

"Quick and painless?" I smirk, knowing full well it'll be anything but that for Leo.

"Hardly." He puts his spoon down, suddenly pushing the half-eaten bowl away as if his appetite just left the room. "I'll be wrong. I'll have been wrong about *Arborville*. I've never been wrong before. I've always been the guy who could pull it off. Always. Now, I'm...not." He shakes his head, almost shuddering. "I'm not quite used to that yet. I'm not sure I want to get used to it."

I grab his hand. "I think Leo Corbin the human might be far better than Leo Corbin the legend. Being wrong isn't fatal."

"It's not fun, I'll tell you that much."

We fall quiet for a moment, pondering the catastrophic shift of events in the last twenty-four hours. It dawns on me, quietly at first but then with a little more sparkle, that there is only one thing to say. Only one real balm, one real antidote. "I love you."

Leo takes my hand and brings it to his lips. He plants a tender kiss there, then holds my hand to his cheek.

"I'll love you after today is over," I go on, "and tomorrow and I'm pretty sure about the day after that. I'll love you if you can't save a single show next season."

Leo's eyes fall shut and I feel him press my hand. He doesn't say anything, and he doesn't have to. His touch, and the look on his face, they say it all for him. I'm sitting there, smiling at him, when he wordlessly gets up, slides over to my side of the booth, and kisses me. "I love you," he whispers, and it tingles out to my fingertips. He kisses me again. "I love you," Leo repeats, louder this time. He does it a third time, and people around us begin whooping and applauding. By the fourth round, the entire restaurant is staring at us, clapping, yelling "Atta boy!" and other less delicate remarks.

I'm turning scarlet. I can feel the flush creep up my neck in what is surely ugly, uncinematic blotches. Leo, on the other hand, is laughing. He pulls up out of the booth, bringing me along with him. He makes a big, sweeping bow, sending the crowd into whoops and whistles over the still-constant applause. Despite the fact that I would rather be hiding under the booth table right now, Leo grabs me by the waist and tugs me down into a bow with him. The crowd goes wild. With another sound kiss, he tosses a twenty-dollar bill on the table, extends a genteel elbow, and escorts me out of the restaurant as if we were walking up the red carpet at Grauman's Chinese Theater.

Chapter Twenty-Eight

The alternative happy ending

"He loves her, she loves him, enter the happy ending, right?" Suzann pours me another cup of coffee while brushing her hair. I should have gone home to sleep—and I will, soon—but I needed to talk to Suzann more than I needed to sleep and she goes to work soon. You have to love a friend who'll let you bang on her door at 5:00 a.m. so you can drink her coffee and spill your guts while she's trying to get ready for work.

"I'm happy," I reply, "but it's sure not ending. It's just starting."

Suzan stops brushing and stares at me. "Are you? Happy I mean?"

"Yeah," I yawn, "it feels like it."

"Think about that, Lindy. Your job's falling apart around your ankles and you're *happy.*" She glares at me, a *and the moral of this story is?* look in her eyes.

"I'm too tired to draw meaningful conclusions. Make your point."

"You are not your job, Lindy. Maggie can't make you happy, but maybe Leo can."

I straighten in my chair. "Hey, I know that. Aren't I always the one who's said 'Maggie is what I do, not who I am'?"

"Congratulations," Suz replies, "I think you finally believe it."

"I've always believed it. I broke it off with Kyle because of it." We're toeing up to the boundaries of acceptable best-friend lecturing here.

"Kyle got creepy, I'll grant you that, but you broke it off with him because you were falling for Leo. And, kiddo, I've a news bulletin for you: One of the reasons you fell for Leo is because he *already knew.* There was no secret to reveal. You've been rating every guy on how he reacts to Maggie, and you finally found someone who doesn't give a hoot about Maggie."

We've crossed the boundaries. "That's not true!" But, don't you know, the minute the words leave my mouth I remember my thoughts while yarn-hunting at Fiber Content. I wince. "Mostly."

Suzann parks one hand on her hip. Even in a bathrobe, she can nail you with her eyes. "Okay, so why do *you* think it is you've never dated anyone from inside the industry?"

"Because they're all weirdos?" I make a face at her. The woman is so infuriatingly…right.

"Because you have no trump card with them, no escape clause. Because they might dump you without your cool job. You hate the Maggie-izers, but you're really terrified of the people who couldn't care less about Maggie, because they just might really love *you*." She puts both elbows down on her kitchen counter and leans in toward me. "*You* for cute, lovable, just-fine-as-an-ordinary person *you*."

I sniffle into my coffee. "I will not

dignify that tender remark by crying. I'm tired and emotional, that's all. But I love you anyway." I look up at her, wiping the back of my hand across my eyes. "I thought you didn't like Leo."

"I was suspicious of Leo. There's a difference. I think the guy's proved himself. Of course, I will require a full interrogation before I grant my final approval. I can't have just anybody escorting my maid of honor to my wedding—I've got standards."

I rest my chin in my hand. "I love him, Suz."

"I know." She smiles.

"I'm terrified."

"I know. God knows, too. Between the three of you, I have a feeling you'll get it all worked out in the end."

"Amen." I say, letting my head fall to the counter.

Suz kisses the back of my head like a mom. "I gotta go to work, hon. What are you going to do now?"

"Sleep, more sleep, then go see about Marilyn."

Suz stops on her way out of the kitchen and looks back at me. "The lizard?"

"Someone's gotta take care of her while Nigel's in the hospital."

"You're right," she calls as she pads down the hall. "You industry types *are* all weirdos."

Standing in Nigel's apartment later that day, tending to Marilyn and picking up the mess all over, my heart continues to ache for that tornado of a man. I pick up a T-shirt, I pray for the heart once inside it. *It's broken, Lord, in a dozen different ways. But that's where You reach people best, isn't it? Nigel matters to You. Would You take* Arborville *from him if that's what it took to get his attention?*

It is there that the real question strikes me. *Would You take* Arborville *from me if that's what it took to get mine? Is Suzann right?*

I know the answer. The Lord who gave His only Son for me would do whatever it took to pull my wandering heart back toward Him. Not that I see God as a big bully, taking away my treasures to make me miserable. I see it more as a loving parent, taking my face in His hands and saying "Look at Me. Not the other stuff you think makes you happy, but focus on Me."

Am I glad *Arborville*'s going down? Not a bit. Am I scared I'll never have an opportunity like this again? You bet. Terrified.

Am I going to be okay? I'm starting to think so.

Is Leo going to be okay? I'll let you know. I've got to go home and grab a few hours of sleep. Leo's got to go home, shave, spend an hour or two working up documents on his computer and go into the office for the meeting that will change his life.

Actually, I don't think that's true. I think Leo will discover life with a defeat isn't the end of the world. I think God has some refocusing planned for Leo, too. Sophia says it's our mistakes that teach us how to knit better. That we learn far more from the flawed projects than we do from the fun ones.

She was right about Nigel, too, wasn't she?

Oh, and speaking of yarn, you'll never guess what happened when Leo dropped me off last night—this morning. My green-brown sweater was still out in the middle of the floor where I stepped on it. Leo picked it up and asked what it was.

I made up some short answer about it being a sweater I botched—not untrue, but certainly not the full answer. I tried to distract him—tried to take it out of his hands, even, but he kept looking at it.

"I like it." He said. "The brown's the color of your eyes."

Wow.

Never, in the *entire time* I was working that sweater, did I realize the brown is not only the color of Kyle's eyes, but the color of mine.

The yarn really *does* know.

But right now, I'm cleaning Nigel's apartment for him. Even though I know he's got people for this, I want to be the one to do it. I want to offer him a bit of order, to let him come home to calm even though his world is spinning out of control. Or spinning back into focus—depends on how you look at it. Depends on how Nigel looks at it, too.

As I'm throwing pizza box number four into the garbage, my cell rings. It's Leo.

"Hi there. You okay?"

"I will be," he replies, his voice strained. "When can I see you?"

"How about right now? Griffith Park? We can go up to the observatory and just sit."

Leo sighs on the other end. "Sounds like heaven. You at Nigel's or something?"

"Just seeing to Marilyn and a few other things."

"Do me a favor?"

Leo could ask me for the moon today and I'd try and get it for him. "Anything."

"Leave the lizard at home?"

"Relax," I laugh. "From here on in, there won't be anything between us."

Epilogue

The happy couple in lane six

Four straight gutter balls. You'd think I can do better than that. Especially in this dress.

Leo, however, seems to bowl best in formalwear. After Suzann's spectacular wedding today, it seemed the only place to burn off the postreception calories was Ten Pin. After all, we do have a bit of history with the place.

Sure, we got looks when we walked in—Leo in a tux, me in my red shimmery bridesmaid's dress. At least this time I matched my ball. Dino stared down the other customers on our behalf and gave us the best lane. Dino's a good guy. Maybe now that Nigel's in rehab and took his Bible with him, Dino will be my new project. He's got a big heart. Jesus could do amazing things through him. After all, the season wraps up in four episodes and I'll be looking for things to do.

"Lost your edge?" Leo teases as he marks an oversize zero on the scorecard. "I hope you nailed your call-back audition yesterday better than you nailed that last frame." My consolation prize is a tender little kiss on the back of my neck as I wait for my ball to return. I've been getting smooches with every frame, come to think of it.

"Maybe I'm just letting you win. Protecting your tender male ego and all."

Leo puffs up his chest. "Maybe I'm just too distracting in all my dashing tuxedoness. Those girls over there were staring at me earlier."

I throw him a look. "You're bowling in a tux. They're staring because you look weird, not dashing."

"Hey, *my* shoes match at least." He stomps his tall frame over to me and stares me down.

I stick my chin out and plant a hand on one hip. "You're the one who forgot to buy me decent shoes. You started the whole bowling thing, remember?"

"Yeah," Leo sighs, pulling me into his arms. "Just look what we started. Who'd have known?" He kisses my forehead, and my eyes fall shut at his touch. "I love you, Lindy."

"I love you, too." I get another kiss. I'm really starting to like bowling.

A familiar voice booms over the loudspeaker. "Will the happy couple in lane six kindly get *on with it?*"

"Trust me," Leo answers quietly, looking straight into my eyes, "I plan to."

* * * * *

Dear Reader, ·

It's a funny thing we writers do. How many other people get talking owls popping up in their imaginations? Or bejeweled iguanas? I love that God lets me giggle through my imagination. I'm honored that I get to share that wonder with you.

Lindy and Leo tackle truths we all confront: that life takes U-turns, but God never turns away from us. Even when it feels life is falling down around our ankles, we can place our hope in the strength and perfection of God's plan. I hope you gain a stronger sense of God's trustworthiness from reading Leo and Lindy's story. I pray you learned how to rethink your own story—because all of our stories are so very far from finished. We're all "in progress" and "in transformation," even when it feels like we're "in trouble."

I saw a sign on a store cash register once that read Don't Be Afraid Of The Future—God Is Already There. It's a truth we can never hear too many times.

Many thanks for reading, and as always, I'd love to hear from you. Come visit www.alliepleiter.com and drop me a digital line (or your favorite knitting pattern or chocolate recipe!). If pen and paper is more your thing, drop me a note at P.O. Box 7026, Villa Park, IL 60181.

Blessings to each and every one of you,

QUESTIONS FOR DISCUSSION:

1. What would be your "dream job"? Take a moment and daydream about what your life would be like if you had that job. What is it that captures your heart? Can you think of any downsides?

2. Do you have a favorite cartoon character? Who is it and why do you think that character appeals so much to you?

3. How do you relate to Lindy's distrust of Leo's motives early in the book? Would you rate her suspicions as justified or not? Where does faith help us overcome doubts? What role does personal integrity play?

4. Do you have a Nigel in your life—someone who needs faith but can't seem to grasp it? What helps you persist with them? What makes it so difficult?

5. Lindy soothes her spirit with knitting. What soothes your spirit? If you need to find something, what do you think it might be?

6. Lindy's job became "the thing she loved the most." What could become that thing for you? Take an honest stock of what is nearest and dearest to you. Do your priorities need realignment?

7. Sometimes great clarity comes with a great crisis. Think back to a time when your life seemed in upheaval. What did you learn?

8. If you were in Lindy's shoes, would you have given Kyle another chance? Why or why not?

9. Lindy found it hard to trust that God had a future for her beyond Arborville. Where are you finding it hard to trust God? How did Lindy's story help to strengthen your trust?